Reviving Legacy

by

A.D. Curtis

Bourbon Bloodline

Cover Art by *Lea Schizas*

The Wild Rose Press, Inc.
PO Box 708
Adams Basin, NY 14410-0708
Visit us at www.thewildrosepress.com

Publishing History
First Edition, 2025
Trade Paperback ISBN 978-1-5092-6227-4
Digital ISBN 978-1-5092-6228-1

Bourbon Bloodline
Published in the United States of America

Dedication

To my sons, Colson and Brody,

May you always chase your dreams with courage, love with all your hearts, and never stop believing in the magic of your own potential. You both are my world, my heart, my all. I love you both to the moon and back!

Thank you for believing in me and supporting this unbelievable journey!

Chapter 1

The sun dipped low in the sky, casting golden light across the lush fields of Bourbon County as Grayson and Knox Beaumont approached their ancestral home. The imposing structure of Beaumont Manor loomed before them, its stone walls steeped in history and shadows. Grayson's piercing blue-gray eyes swept over the familiar surroundings, taking in the ivy-clad exterior and the carefully tended gardens that hinted at the secrets within.

"Feels like a lifetime since we've been here," Grayson murmured, his voice tinged with nostalgia.

"More than one, actually," Knox replied, his deep brown eyes betraying a hint of amusement at his brother's understatement. Together, they climbed the steps to the grand entrance, their footsteps echoing through the empty space as they pushed open the heavy oak doors.

"Welcome home, Master Grayson, Master Knox," came the refined voice of Winston "Wixx" Beaumont, the loyal caretaker who had maintained the manor in their absence. His tall, lean frame was clad in a tailored suit, and he executed a formal bow with practiced grace.

"Thank you, Wixx," Grayson said with a warm smile, momentarily distracted by the quiet strength in Wixx's salt-and-pepper gaze. "It's good to be back."

"Indeed, it is an honor to have you both return," Wixx replied, his tone filled with reverence for the brothers he had served for so many years.

As they stepped further into the grand entrance, Grayson couldn't help but feel a sense of homecoming wash over him. Despite the countless places he'd traveled and the endless years that stretched out behind him, there was something about the manor that stirred the deepest parts of his soul. It was a connection born of blood and legacy, one that he knew Knox shared.

"Your accommodations have been prepared, and I have seen to it that all is in order for your stay," Wixx continued, his eyes filled with a loyalty that was both humbling and reassuring.

"Thank you, Wixx," Knox said quietly, his gaze lingering on the details of the entrance hall as if committing them to memory. His thoughts were already turning to the secrets they had come to uncover, and the knowledge that would help them revive their family's legacy.

"Shall I show you around, Masters?" Wixx offered, his voice steady and sure as he gestured toward the grand staircase that led to the upper floors.

"Please do," Grayson replied, his tone light and playful, despite the weight of their purpose. "It's been so long since we've seen these hallowed halls."

"Very well, Masters," Wixx said with a nod, his expression betraying a hint of pride as he prepared to lead them through the manor. He knew the importance of their mission and the role he played in securing the future of the Beaumont family. And as the brothers followed him deeper into the heart of the manor, they couldn't help but feel the past reaching out to embrace them, welcoming them back into the fold of their intriguing destiny.

The soft glow of the chandelier cast shadows across the entrance hall, illuminating the elaborate wallpaper and ornate moldings that adorned the walls. Grayson couldn't help but smile at the sight, feeling a surge of nostalgia for the days when he and Knox would race down the grand staircase, laughter echoing through the manor.

"Tell me, Wixx," Grayson said, his tone playful as he glanced at the caretaker with a mischievous glint in his eyes, "have you always had such impeccable taste, or is it a gift that has only improved with age?"

Wixx's lips curved into the faintest of smiles, his piercing blue eyes twinkling beneath the weight of Grayson's teasing. "I have made it my life's work to maintain the beauty and character of this estate, Master Grayson," he replied, his voice filled with warmth despite its formal cadence. "It is an honor to serve the Beaumont family."

"Indeed," Grayson mused, his gaze traveling over the intricate details of the hall, each one a testament to Wixx's dedication. "I can see that every corner of this place has been cared for with great devotion."

Knox, standing off to the side, remained quiet during the exchange, his deep brown eyes scanning the room with a keen, almost hungry intensity. Though he said nothing, he nodded in acknowledgment of Wixx's presence, the subtle gesture conveying his gratitude for the caretaker's unwavering loyalty.

As Grayson continued to banter playfully with Wixx, he felt a bittersweet pang of longing for the simpler times before immortality had transformed their lives. The familiar sights and smells of the manor tugged at his heart, stirring up memories of laughter, love, and loss.

In the silence of his own thoughts, Knox could not help but reflect on the changes that had taken place since their departure. The passage of time was evident in the subtle wear on the wallpaper and the slightly dimmed luster of the chandelier crystals. He wondered if, like the manor itself, his own heart bore the invisible scars of time's relentless march.

"Your family would be proud of your return, Masters," Wixx said softly, his voice carrying a note of reverence as he regarded Grayson and Knox. "The legacy of the Beaumont name is destined to rise once more."

"Thank you, Wixx," Grayson murmured, his eyes meeting the caretaker's in a moment of shared understanding. "We will not let our ancestors down."

Wixx's polished shoes tapped rhythmically against the marble floor as he led Grayson and Knox through the sprawling manor, each footstep echoing like a distant memory. The fading light from the setting sun filtered through the stained-glass windows, casting an ethereal glow on the walls adorned with ancestral portraits. Grayson followed closely behind, his senses awash with nostalgia, as their caretaker recounted tales of the family's past.

"Ah, here we have the ballroom," Wixx declared, gesturing toward an ornate set of double doors that opened onto a grand space filled with shadows and echoes of bygone revelry. "Many a suitor has danced the night away beneath those gilded chandeliers, vying for the hearts of Beaumont debutantes."

"Indeed, I recall quite a few scandalous waltzes in my time," Grayson replied with a wicked grin, his mind flooding with memories of stolen kisses and feverish trysts. He felt a surge of longing, both for the pleasures of his past and hope for his future.

Knox listened intently to Wixx's stories, his stoic expression betraying no emotion, though the weight of their family history pressed heavily upon him. As they continued their tour, Grayson couldn't help but notice the tension that seemed to coil around his brother like a snake, constricting his every breath.

"Here, Masters," Wixx said, opening another door to reveal a dimly lit music room. Dust motes danced in the air, swirling like ancient spirits around the grand piano that dominated one corner.

Grayson's eyes sparkled with delight at the sight, drawn irresistibly to the ebony instrument that held so many cherished memories. He approached it reverently, his fingers aching to caress the ivory keys once more. With a sigh, he lifted the fallboard and allowed his fingers to glide over the keys, coaxing forth a haunting melody that seemed to resonate with the very essence of their family's legacy.

As the notes swirled through the air, Grayson felt a deep connection to both the past and present. The music was a bridge between the two, a reminder of all they had lost and all they still had to gain. He glanced at Knox, hoping that his brother could sense the same unity within the lilting tune.

"Gray," Knox whispered, his voice tinged with emotion as he acknowledged the beauty and power of the moment. "I can feel our ancestors in this room, urging us forward."

"Then let us honor them, brother, by reviving our legacy and embracing the world that fate has granted us," Grayson replied, his eyes gleaming with determination and a newfound sense of purpose.

With the final chord still lingering in the air, the brothers shared a nod, silently vowing to uphold their family's name and seize the happiness that had so long eluded them. As they prepared to leave the music room, Grayson looked back at the grand piano, its ebony surface now glowing softly with the promise of a brighter future.

The flickering glow of a solitary candle cast dancing shadows across the library's towering shelves, as if the very souls of the Beaumont ancestors were reaching out from the dusty stacks. The scent of aged leather and parchment hung heavy in the air, mingling with the lingering aroma of bourbon that seemed to permeate every corner of the manor.

"Knox," Grayson murmured, his voice ever so low with the soft creaking of floorboards beneath their feet, "can you feel it?"

"Feel what?" Knox replied, his deep brown eyes flitting between the rows of ancient books, each one holding centuries of wisdom and secrets. He ran his fingers along the spines, deliberate and reverent, as though he could absorb the knowledge hidden within simply by touch.

"The stories of our ancestors," Grayson continued, the haunting melody from the music room still echoing in his heart. "Their love, their pain, their sacrifices–it's all here, waiting for us to uncover."

"Yes," Wixx chimed in, his voice rich with reverence. "And there is one story in particular that I believe you will find most intriguing."

The brothers exchanged a glance, curiosity awakened, before following Wixx through the library's labyrinthine depths. With each step, the weight of the past pressed down upon them, awakening memories long buried and igniting a hunger for lost knowledge.

Finally, they entered the family's private study, where a single shaft of moonlight illuminated an unassuming leather-bound book resting on a polished mahogany desk. Grayson drew closer, his blue-gray eyes widening with recognition as he traced a finger over the faded gold lettering: Beaumont Bourbon Recipes.

"Father's old recipe book," he whispered, the words sounding like a prayer. "I thought this was lost to time."

"Nothing is ever truly lost," Wixx replied, a hint of a smile touching his lips. "Merely waiting to be rediscovered."

"Then let us begin," Knox announced, his stoic demeanor cracking to reveal a spark of excitement. "Together, we shall breathe new life into these forgotten secrets and restore our family's legacy to its rightful place."

As they gathered around the book, Grayson couldn't help but feel a surge of desire course through him. This was more than just a collection of recipes—it was their birthright, their heritage, and the key to a future where both love and ambition could flourish.

"Here's to the journey ahead," he whispered, his heart swelling with pride as he glanced at Knox and Wixx, the two most important people in his life. "And to the untold stories that await us."

Grayson's fingers trembled as they grazed the worn leather cover of the recipe book, a sense of reverence and awe flooding his senses. He felt as if he were standing on the edge of something monumental—the resurrection of a once-great legacy that now lay dormant in the pages before him.

"Can you imagine it, Knox?" Grayson asked, his voice hushed with excitement as he flipped through the pages. "The possibilities that lie within these pages…It's like we're holding the key to our family's salvation."

Knox, ever the meticulous one, pulled out a notebook from his jacket pocket, his deep brown eyes scanning the pages with a quiet intensity. "Indeed," he murmured, his pen poised above the paper. "But we must approach this with caution and precision. The slightest miscalculation could prove disastrous."

"Of course," Grayson agreed, his eyes sparkling with anticipation. "But think of the reward, brother. Our name will once again be synonymous with the finest bourbon in Kentucky."

As Grayson continued to peruse the recipes, his mind began to race with visions of grandeur—ornate bottles filled with liquid gold lining the shelves of their restored distillery, the scent of aging oak barrels permeating the air, and the renewed respect of their peers as they reclaimed their rightful place among the elite.

A particular recipe caught Grayson's eye, and he traced the faded ink with a delicate touch, absorbing the intricate blend of ingredients and techniques. "This one," he whispered, more to himself than anyone else. "There's something about it that feels…special."

"Let me see," Knox said, leaning in closer to examine the page. His brow furrowed in concentration as he studied the text, his pen scribbling notes in the margin of his notebook. "It does seem rather unique. Perhaps it could be the cornerstone of our revival."

"Exactly," Grayson replied, a wolfish grin spreading across his face. "The beginning of a new era for the Beaumont name."

Their excitement was recognizable, a living entity that seemed to pulse through the room like electricity. Grayson's heart raced in his chest, fueled by a potent mix of adrenaline and desire. He could practically taste the success that now lay tantalizingly within reach, and he yearned to seize it with both hands.

"Let's not waste any more time, then," Knox said, snapping his notebook shut with a sense of finality. "We have much work ahead of us."

"Yes, we do," Grayson replied, his voice thick with determination. "Together, we will ensure that our family's legacy is not only revived but also surpasses anything our ancestors could have ever imagined."

As they stood side by side in the dimly lit study, their shared resolve radiating like a beacon in the darkness, Grayson couldn't help but feel as if this was the moment when everything would change—for better or worse. But one thing was certain: they would face whatever challenges lay ahead, together and united by the indomitable spirit of the Beaumont bloodline.

The fading embers of the fireplace cast a warm, golden glow on the ancient leather-bound book as Grayson and Knox exchanged a glance, their eyes reflecting a silent understanding that seemed to shimmer in the air between them. Their determination to succeed in their mission was palpable, like a living, breathing entity that pulsed to the rhythm of their immortal hearts.

"Ready?" Grayson asked, his voice low and steady, laced with the steel of resolve.

"Always," Knox replied, his eyes never leaving Grayson's as they closed the book in unison, a symbolic gesture marking the beginning of their journey.

As if drawn by the magnetic force of their shared purpose, Wixx stepped forward, his keen intuition sensing the brothers' unwavering commitment. In his elegant hands, he held the last remaining bottle of Beaumont Bourbon–a relic from a bygone era, now poised to herald the rebirth of their family's legacy. Sure, the distillery still ran, but the bourbon it produced was not this, but one day, it would again.

"May I propose a toast?" Wixx suggested, his voice filled with reverence as he uncorked the bottle, the rich aroma of aged oak and caramel drifting through the room like a whispered promise of the wonders yet to come.

"Please do, Wixx," Grayson replied, his blue-gray eyes flickering with anticipation as the caretaker poured the amber liquid into three crystal glasses, each one chiming softly as it met the polished surface of the mahogany table.

"Very well," Wixx began, raising his glass and holding Grayson's gaze. "To your success, gentlemen. May the past guide your steps toward a future of triumph and prosperity."

"Cheers," the brothers echoed, lifting their glasses to join Wixx's in a chorus of crystalline notes that seemed to resonate through the very walls of Beaumont

Manor.

As the bourbon passed his lips, Grayson couldn't help but close his eyes, savoring the rich, velvety taste of their heritage. Each sip was a testament to the potential that lay within them–a reminder of the indomitable spirit that had birthed their family's legacy and now burned brighter than ever within their souls.

"Thank you, Wixx," Knox said, his deep voice resonating with genuine gratitude as he set his glass down on the table. "We won't let our ancestors down."

"Or ourselves," Grayson added, his mind already dancing with visions of the bourbon they would create—a symphony of flavors that would not only revive their family's name but also cement their place in history.

"Yes, sir," Wixx agreed, his eyes shining with pride and loyalty. "I have every confidence in your abilities, gentlemen. The Beaumont name will rise once more, I am certain of it."

With that, the trio shared one last look, each man keenly aware of the gravity of the task that lay before them and the unbreakable bond that united them in this sacred endeavor. As the brothers turned to leave, the weight of their ancestral home seemed to settle on their shoulders, a mantle of responsibility that they bore with stoic grace and unwavering determination.

"Let the journey begin," Grayson whispered, his words a solemn vow that would echo through the halls of Beaumont Manor for centuries to come.

The clink of crystal glasses resonated through the dimly lit study, like an ancient melody that echoed the spirit of the Beaumont family. Grayson's blue-gray eyes met Knox's deep brown gaze as they raised their glasses in unison.

"To our ancestors," Grayson declared, his voice laced with determination and a quiet reverence. "And to our future."

"Cheers," Knox responded, a hint of a smile tugging at the corners of his lips as he acknowledged their shared purpose.

As the brothers took another sip, the rich taste of their family's history enveloped them, each nuance of flavor awakening long-dormant memories and stirring strong emotions within them. Grayson closed his eyes, allowing the bourbon to tantalize his senses, while Knox savored every note, his mind already dissecting the complexities of their ancestors' craftsmanship.

"Exquisite," Grayson murmured, his voice low and filled with passion. "Our family truly was unparalleled in their skill."

"There is no doubt in that," Knox agreed, his tone reflective. "But we'll surpass them, Grayson. We'll create something even more extraordinary."

Grayson's lips curved into a mischievous grin. "I wouldn't have it any other way, brother."

Their glasses now empty, the air between them hummed with newfound resolve and anticipation. They both knew the road ahead would be fraught with challenges, but there was no turning back now.

"Thank you, Wixx," Grayson said sincerely, placing a hand on the caretaker's shoulder, his eyes gleaming with gratitude. "You welcoming us home means more to us than you can imagine."

Wixx inclined his head, his voice thick with emotion. "It is my honor to serve the Beaumont family, now and always."

"Rest well, Wixx," Knox added, his expression softening for just a moment. "We'll need your guidance and expertise as we journey through the estate tomorrow."

"Of course, gentlemen," Wixx replied, his chest swelling with pride. "I shall be at your disposal, as always."

With that, Grayson and Knox bid Wixx goodnight, their footsteps echoing against the hardwood floors as they made their way to their respective rooms. The shadows of the past loomed around them, yet their hearts were filled with a fierce determination to forge a new legacy and claim their place among the annals of Bourbon County history.

The moon cast its silvery glow upon the lush gardens of Beaumont Manor, casting elongated shadows that seemed to dance in tandem with the flickering flames of the gas lanterns lining the hallway. Grayson and Knox walked side by side, their footsteps resounding in sync with the measured ticking of an ancient grandfather clock that had borne witness to centuries of secrets.

"Can you believe it, Knox?" Grayson murmured, his voice tinged with a mix of nostalgia and anticipation. "We're finally back to where it all began."

Knox's lips curved into a slight smile, his eyes gleaming with a quiet determination. "Indeed, brother," he replied, his tone measured but betraying a hint of excitement. "This is just the beginning, though. We have much to learn, much to uncover."

As they approached their respective bedroom doors, Grayson paused for a moment, his fingers brushing against the cool brass doorknob. In his mind's eye, he saw the rows of charred oak barrels nestled within the depths of their family's aging cellar, each one filled with a unique blend of bourbon that held the promise of revitalizing the Beaumont name. The intoxicating scent of caramel and toasted vanilla enveloped him, beckoning him to immerse himself in the artistry of his ancestors.

"Gray," Knox whispered, his fingers hovering over the ancient books on his bedside table, "we will breathe new life into our legacy. Together, we will weave the tapestry of our past into an even richer future."

"Yes," Grayson agreed, his voice low as the weight of their mission settled on his shoulders. He could almost feel the warm embrace of a normal human life around him, urging him forward toward the tantalizing unknown. But he knew that he had to focus on the task that lay before them. Stay on track, or he may never reach his goal.

"Goodnight, Knox," Grayson murmured, his fingers lingering on the door handle as if grasping onto the last vestiges of the past.

"Goodnight, Gray," Knox replied, his voice a soothing balm to Grayson's frayed nerves. "Tomorrow, we take the first step toward reclaiming our destiny."

With a nod and a shared glance filled with unspoken understanding, they each entered their chambers, the doors closing softly behind them. As Grayson drifted into sleep, his dreams were haunted by visions of golden amber liquid swirling in crystal glasses. Meanwhile, Knox's thoughts turned to ancient alchemical texts and arcane secrets, each one a potential key to unlocking the full potential of the Beaumont bourbon legacy.

Together, bound by blood and loyalty, Grayson and Knox embarked on a journey to restore their family's honor and rekindle the smoldering embers of a passion that defied the constraints of time and mortality. And as the sun rose on the next day, the brothers got busy planning a party. Time to reintroduce the Beaumont name to the high society of Bourbon County.

The following morning, the sun streamed through the manor's stately windows, casting long beams of light on the antique furniture. The scent of freshly brewed coffee wafted from the kitchen, stirring Grayson from his deep slumber. His azure-gray eyes blinked open, and for a moment his gaze lingered on the intricate ceiling, awash with gilded plasterwork. Taking a deep breath, he pushed back the heavy silk sheets and swung his legs over the edge of the bed.

A day full of promise lay ahead, the first in their long journey to restore their family's honor.

Across the hall, Knox was already awake; he had been for hours. Sitting at his mahogany desk in front of an array of dog-eared notebooks filled with notes on distillation techniques, alchemical processes, and obscure bourbon recipes. His mind was a whirlpool of ideas and calculations as his fingers gripped an antique fountain pen with a sense of resolve.

After sharing a hasty breakfast, prepared by Wixx, who still refused to let them lift a finger in the kitchen despite their protests, Grayson and Knox made their way to the study. Its grand bookshelves housed generations of knowledge about bourbon-making—a testament to their family's enduring pursuit of perfection.

"Are you ready for this?" Grayson asked Knox as

he turned toward him, his gaze intense and unyielding.

"As ready as ever," Knox replied simply, although his tone betrayed a hint of uncertainty that went unnoticed by his brother.

They spent most of the day poring over old documents and books filled with meticulous instructions and cryptic annotations left by their forebears. But as evening fell and shadows lengthened across Bourbon County, it was clear they needed more than just their ancestors' wisdom to succeed.

In between sifting through piles of ancient parchment and dusty books, they organized a lavish soirée scheduled for a week from that day. A grand event to announce the return of the Beaumont brothers to high society and their reclamation of the family's bourbon legacy.

Grayson took charge of planning the event, his talent for charming and entertaining guests coming to the fore. He ordered thousands of twinkling fairy lights to drape over the manor's façade, and the ballroom was scrubbed and polished until it glistened in the sunlight. An orchestra was hired to play soft jazz throughout the night, and Wixx was tasked with preparing the finest selection of hors d'oeuvres Bourbon County had ever seen.

As preparations for the event continued, word quickly traveled through Bourbon County about the impending return of the Beaumonts. Excitement bubbled among high society; whispers of anticipation echoed through parlors and drawing rooms, stoked by Grayson's infectious energy.

A new chapter was about to be written in the annals of Bourbon County, and at the heart of it all were two men who would defy all odds for the sake of their inheritance.

When the day finally arrived, it was warm, with a balmy breeze that rustled through the verdant foliage of the estate, carrying with it the sweet fragrance of blooming magnolias, the brother's late grandmother Ravenna's favorite of all the flowers and trees on the estate. A flurry of preparations were underway, as lavish drapes were drawn back, revealing tall, arched windows that flooded the grand ballroom with soft, filtered sunlight. The air buzzed with an electric sense of anticipation as maids and butlers scurried around under Wixx's stern gaze, readying the mansion for an event that would surely become the talk of Bourbon County.

Grayson stood at the top of the sweeping staircase that led down to the foyer, his sharp ocean eyes scanning the opulent expanse below. His tailored suit accentuated his athletic build, and his dark hair was styled to perfection. But beneath his confident exterior, a knot of apprehension coiled tightly in his stomach. This wasn't just a party; it was their reentry into a world they had left behind almost a century ago.

Beside him, Knox seemed deep in thought, his chestnut eyes distant. "This is it, Gray," he murmured, his voice barely audible over the sound of clinking glasses and laughter that spilled from the open doors. "We're about to open our lives to them again."

"I know," Grayson replied quietly. He slipped a hand into his pocket and pulled out an old pocket-watch—a relic from their grandfather's time and now one of their few tangible connections to their past. "But we're not those boys anymore," he said, turning it over in his hands.

"No," Knox agreed after a moment's silence. "We're much more."

As evening fell, lanterns flickered to life, casting dancing shadows across the sprawling lawns. The strains of a jazz quartet wafted through the air, mingling with the aroma of roasting meats and aged bourbon. A stream of classic cars began to arrive, their gleaming bodies reflecting the soft glow from the lanterns.

Inside, Grayson and Knox descended the grand staircase, their entrance drawing a collective gasp from their guests. This was indeed a new chapter for the Beaumont Brothers, one that promised intrigue, excitement and perhaps…love?

Chapter 2

The grand ballroom of Beaumont Manor was awash in a golden glow, the twinkling chandeliers casting their warm light upon the lively gathering below. A soft jazz melody played by a live band filled the air, blending harmoniously with the hum of laughter and conversation. Grayson and Knox Beaumont moved effortlessly through the crowd, their imposing figures drawing admiring glances from the guests as they mingled with Bourbon County's elite.

"Grayson, my boy," a silver-haired man greeted them, his eyes alight with genuine warmth. He was Richard Thornton, one of the most prominent racehorse owners in the county. "It's been too long since we've had any Beaumont's at one of these functions."

"Indeed, it has, Richard," Grayson replied, his blue-gray eyes glinting with mischief. "We thought it was high time we introduced ourselves to society and reintroduce the Beaumont name." A subtle tension hung between the brothers, a silent understanding of the true nature they concealed beneath their charming facades.

"Ah, and what better way than to host such a marvelous event," gushed a woman beside Richard. She was Eleanor Clay, wife of a local bourbon magnate. Her wine-red gown shimmered as she gestured with her champagne flute. "Your family's estate is simply breathtaking, Grayson."

"Thank you, Eleanor," Grayson said, his voice smooth as the aged bourbon he had grown up drinking. "We wanted to make sure our guests felt welcome and comfortable."

As they conversed with the various guests—bourbon makers, politicians, and other influential figures—Grayson couldn't help but feel a strange sense of anticipation, as though something or someone was about to change the course of the night.

And then she entered.

Raven Ballard appeared in the doorway like an enchantress stepping out of a dream, her raven-black hair cascading down her back in soft waves. Her emerald eyes seemed to shift in hue, reflecting the chandeliers' golden light and casting an otherworldly allure upon her flawless skin.

Her graceful movement captivated everyone as she gracefully made her way through the crowd. By her side were her two best friends, Marley La Rue and Madison Carter, their close bond evident in the way they moved in sync, forming a united front as they navigated the bustling room.

"Who is that?" Grayson found himself asking Eleanor, unable to tear his gaze away from Raven's captivating presence.

"Ah, that's Raven Ballard," Eleanor replied, following his gaze. "She owns the Witch's Brew distillery, one of the finest bourbons in the county, and possibly the state."

As Grayson watched Raven approach, he felt an inexplicable pull toward her, his anticipation now focused solely on the alluring woman who had entered his world.

Grayson's gaze remained fixed on Raven as her lithe form moved gracefully through the crowd, her emerald eyes sparkling like gems in the chandelier light. He felt an undeniable attraction to her—one that seemed to shimmer in the air between them, electric and alive. Beside him, Knox's own eyes followed Raven with equal fascination, their shared interest silently acknowledged with a subtle raise of an eyebrow and a knowing glance.

"Knox," Grayson murmured, his voice low but determined, "I need to meet her."

"Go ahead," Knox replied, a hint of reluctance in his tone, as he watched his brother prepare to approach the bewitching woman who had captured both their attentions.

As Grayson wove his way through the sea of guests, he couldn't help but feel a sense of wonderment at the magnetic pull that drew him toward Raven. His heart raced with a mixture of excitement and nerves, emotions he hadn't experienced in years.

"Miss Ballard, I presume?" Grayson said, stepping up beside her with a charming smile. Raven turned to face him, her eyes meeting his for the first time—a moment that sent a shiver down Grayson's spine.

"Guilty as charged," she replied, her voice laced with just enough sarcasm to intrigue him further. "And you must be one of the Beaumont brothers, though I must admit I'm not sure which one."

"Grayson," he introduced himself, extending a hand. "It's a pleasure to make your acquaintance."

"Likewise," Raven said, taking his hand with a firm yet delicate grip.

"Your Witch's Brew bourbon has been the talk of

the county," Grayson remarked, gesturing toward the glass cradled in her hand. "I've heard it's quite the transformative experience—much like your entrance this evening."

A faint blush colored Raven's cheeks as she smiled, her eyes narrowing playfully. "Well, Mr. Beaumont, I must say that's quite a compliment. But I'm curious; have you tried it yourself?"

"Alas, I haven't had the pleasure just yet," Grayson admitted, a teasing glint in his eye. "But if it's anything like its creator, I'm sure it's extraordinary."

As their conversation flowed effortlessly, Grayson couldn't help but marvel at how easily Raven held his attention, her wit and intelligence proving to be as intoxicating as the bourbon she crafted. And though he knew he should focus on the purpose of the gathering, he couldn't tear himself away from the magnetic allure of this intriguing woman.

Raven sipped her bourbon, considering Grayson's words with a guarded curiosity. "Extraordinary, you say?" she mused, a sparkle in her emerald eyes. "Well, Mr. Beaumont, I'll have you know that crafting bourbon is an art form. It requires patience, intuition, and a deep understanding of the land from which it hails."

"Indeed," Grayson agreed, his gaze lingering on Raven as if trying to decipher some hidden secret. "I imagine it's not unlike taming a wild stallion or cultivating a delicate rose—all demand a certain finesse and unwavering dedication."

"Exactly," Raven nodded, her passion for her craft evident in the fervor behind her words. Yet, she remained mindful of her surroundings, careful not to reveal too much about herself to this charming stranger.

"Introductions are in order, I believe," Marley La Rue interjected, stepping forward with a friendly smile. "I'm Marley, and this is Madison Carter. We're Raven's best friends and fellow bourbon enthusiasts."

"Ah, fellow connoisseurs," Grayson quipped, inclining his head toward Marley and Madison. "It's a pleasure to meet you both."

"Likewise," Madison said, her eyes glinting with curiosity. "We've heard quite a bit about the Beaumont brothers and their own family bourbon legacy. It seems we share more than a few common interests."

Knox watched the scene unfold from afar, his chestnut hair framing his inscrutable expression. The magnetic pull between his brother and Raven was undeniable, stirring within him a mix of curiosity and hidden emotions he had not felt in years. He longed to approach them, to join the conversation and unravel the mystery that was Raven Ballard, but something held him back—perhaps loyalty to Grayson, or the fear of what might happen if he allowed himself to be drawn into her orbit.

"Yes, we do," Grayson replied, his voice smooth as silk. "And I'm eager to learn more about the magic behind your Witch's Brew bourbon."

"Perhaps another time," Raven said coyly, her eyes never leaving Grayson's as she took another sip of her drink. "After all, I wouldn't want to spoil the surprise for you."

"Very well," Grayson conceded with a playful sigh. "I suppose I'll have to experience it for myself soon enough."

As the conversation flowed around them, Raven

couldn't shake the feeling that someone else was watching her—an intense, almost predatory gaze that seemed to penetrate the very depths of her soul. She glanced around the ballroom, her heart pounding in her chest as she sought the source of this unsettling sensation. And though she spotted Knox Beaumont's dark eyes studying her from across the room, she couldn't quite bring herself to believe that he could be the one responsible for the storm of emotions brewing within her.

Grayson's gaze never left Raven as the lively chatter of the ballroom swirled around them like a whirlwind. He could feel the hum of excitement in the air, the inescapable energy that seemed to emanate from her and draw everyone near. In this moment, he made a decision—one that would change the course of their entwined destinies.

"Would you care to join me for a more private conversation?" Grayson suggested with a charming smile. "There's a quieter corner of the ballroom where we can continue our discussion about Bourbon County and your Witch's Brew without interruption."

Raven hesitated for a heartbeat, her emerald eyes searching his face as if trying to discern his intentions. But then she nodded, the hint of a smile playing at the corners of her lips, and gestured for her friends to accompany her. Grayson led the way through the throng of guests, feeling the weight of Knox's gaze on his back, heavy with unspoken emotions.

As they settled into the secluded corner, the subtle scent of oak and bourbon seemed to wrap around them like a warm embrace. Grayson leaned against the dark wood paneling, watching as Raven and her friends arranged themselves gracefully on a plush velvet settee. There was an intimacy to their shared space that magnified the charged atmosphere between them.

"Tell me," Grayson began, his voice low enough that only their small group could hear. "What inspired you to create Witch's Brew? I've heard whispers of its unique flavor profile, but nothing quite compares to hearing it from the master herself."

Raven seemed to consider his question, her fingers tracing the delicate curves of her glass as her eyes held his. "My grandfather taught me everything I know about bourbon-making," she said softly. "But it was my own affinity for nature that led me to experiment with different techniques and ingredients. I wanted to create something that honored both aspects of my heritage—the rich history of Bourbon County and the magic that flows through its land."

"Ah, so you've tapped into the essence of the land itself," Grayson mused, his interest piqued. "And how does that influence your process? I imagine it's quite different from traditional methods."

"Indeed," Raven agreed with a mysterious smile. "The key lies in timing—aligning the distillation process with the cycles of the moon and the natural energies of the earth. When done correctly, it imbues the bourbon with a subtle, otherworldly quality that 'conventional means can't replicate."

"Your dedication to your craft is truly admirable," Grayson said, genuinely impressed. "I've dabbled in the art of bourbon-making myself, but never have I considered incorporating such mystical elements into the process. It must require a great deal of patience and skill."

Raven tilted her head, her eyes gleaming with curiosity. "And what about you, Grayson? What drew you to Bourbon County? Surely there must be more to your return than a simple desire to revive the family business. For the Beaumonts have not been regulars here in years."

Grayson hesitated for a moment, feeling the weight of his hidden past pressing against his chest like a leaden anchor. But something about Raven's soft gaze, the warmth radiating from her very presence, compelled him to share a piece of his truth.

"Home has always been a complicated concept for me," he admitted, his voice tinged with a melancholy note. "Bourbon County represents not only my family's legacy but also my own search for belonging. In crafting our bourbon, I hope to reconnect with the land and the community—to find some semblance of peace amidst the chaos of the world. After the passing of our grandparents, we felt it was time to take over." Grayson felt the lie stir in him, knowing his actual grandparents had been gone for 50 years or longer. But for now, some truths must remain hidden.

As their conversation deepened, Grayson became increasingly aware of the magnetic pull between them, the smoldering heat that threatened to ignite with every shared word and lingering glance. And though he knew there were so many secrets still hidden in the shadows, secrets that could tear their fragile connection apart, he couldn't help but yearn for more—for the taste of the forbidden fruit that was Raven Ballard.

Knox leaned against a marble pillar, his deep brown eyes following Grayson and Raven as they conversed in the quieter corner of the grand ballroom.

The soft glow of the chandeliers cast shadows on his chiseled features, enhancing the air of brooding mystery that surrounded him. He couldn't deny the pull he felt toward the enchanting woman, her emerald eyes reflecting the flickering candlelight like twin beacons of desire.

"Care to dance?" Grayson asked, offering his hand to Raven with a charming smile, his blue-gray eyes twinkling beneath the golden light.

Raven hesitated for the briefest moment, her gaze darting to Knox before she reluctantly accepted Grayson's offer. "Of course," she replied, her words laced with a subtle hint of uncertainty.

As the sultry strains of a jazz melody filled the air, Grayson led Raven onto the dance floor, their bodies swaying in perfect harmony to the rhythm. Each graceful movement brought them closer, their breaths mingling, the heat between them undeniable.

Knox watched them from the shadows, his heart aching with an intensity that surprised even him. He clenched his fists, fighting the urge to step forward and claim Raven for himself. But his loyalty to his brother held him back, as did the fear of exposing his own supernatural secrets.

"Your dancing is exquisite, Raven," Grayson murmured into her ear, his breath sending shivers down her spine.

"Thank you," she whispered back, her voice barely carried above the music. She couldn't ignore the sparks igniting between them, but something held her back—a sense of caution born from the secrets she harbored within herself.

Their gazes locked, and it seemed as if the rest of

the world faded away, leaving only Grayson and Raven suspended in that single, electric moment. They moved closer still, their lips mere inches apart, the temptation to taste one another's forbidden fruit almost unbearable.

"Grayson," Raven breathed, her voice laced with hesitation. "We can't...I..."

"Shh," he whispered, his thumb brushing against her cheek as he pulled back ever so slightly. "I understand."

Their dance continued, the sensual tension simmering just beneath the surface.

Knox tore his gaze away from the pair, his emotions a tempest raging within him. He knew he should be happy for his brother, yet the sight of Grayson and Raven together only fueled the fire of longing that threatened to consume him.

As the music reached its crescendo, Grayson and Raven shared a final, lingering look, their connection undeniable.

Knox leaned against the ornate marble pillar, his clenched fists hidden in the pockets of his tailored suit as he observed Grayson and Raven from a distance, the chemistry between them was indisputable, their every touch sending sparks through the air that seemed to ignite some long-dormant ember within him.

"Damn it," he muttered under his breath, the weight of his conflicting emotions threatening to crush him. He was torn between loyalty to his brother and the allure of something he hadn't felt in years—an attraction that beckoned like a siren's song, impossible to resist yet fraught with danger.

"Knox, darling, you look positively brooding over here," a sultry voice cooed, snapping him out of his reverie.

His eyes widened as Eva De Young emerged from the shadows, her porcelain skin and piercing amber eyes a stark contrast to the warmth and vitality of the ballroom. Her red lips curved into a teasing smile as she took a step closer, her vintage elegance radiating danger and desire in equal measure.

"Always the observer, aren't you?" Her voice was an intoxicating blend of honey and venom, a challenge wrapped in a seduction. "And who might that be?" She inclined her head subtly toward the dance floor, her gaze following his.

Knox's eyes darkened, an unspoken warning flashing between them. Eva was no stranger to their world.

"Oh, darling, don't be so defensive," Eva purred, her smile widening as she leaned closer until her lips were nearly brushing against his ear. "I'm just curious, that's all."

Despite himself, Knox felt a shudder run down his spine at her proximity. Eva De Young was nothing if not persuasive and he knew better than to underestimate her.

Pulling away from Eva, Knox shot one last glance toward Grayson. In an instant, Grayson was by his brother's side. Tension feeding his very being.

"Hello, Eva," Grayson said cautiously, his voice tight with surprise. "We weren't expecting to see you here."

"Ah, but what is life without little ole me?" Eva purred, her gaze locked on Grayson as if he were the only one in the room. "I couldn't resist when I heard you were back in Kentucky. Thought I would join you all to see what was so important in this, what did you once call it, oh yes, godforsaken country."

Knox watched the exchange, his heart pounding with a mix of dread and discord. He knew all too well the chaos Eva could bring, her obsession with Grayson a dark cloud that had loomed over their lives for decades. And now, just as they were finding solace in the familiar rhythms of Bourbon County, she threatened to tear everything apart once more.

With a wary glance, Raven and her friends cautiously approached the group where Grayson and Knox stood in deep conversation with a striking woman. The air seemed to shift and thicken with an eerie dread as they drew nearer.

"Who's she?" Marley whispered, her gaze locked on Eva. Her normally vibrant eyes held a shadow of uncertainty.

"Trouble," Madison murmured under her breath. Her arm instinctively wrapped around Raven's, a protective gesture.

Raven felt a cold prickle of unease crawl up her spine. She didn't need her witch's instincts to tell her that the woman was dangerous.

Eva's gaze flicked toward them, her amber eyes glinting ominously in the dim light of the ballroom. A knowing smile played on her lips as she turned her attention back to Grayson, slipping an arm through his in a possessive manner that sent a jolt of jealousy through Raven's heart.

Knox watched the interaction from the sidelines, his gut twisting with a mixture of apprehension and resentment. He hated to see Grayson ensnared by Eva's manipulative charm, but even more, he loathed that it was not him who was the focus of Raven's attention.

Raven's emerald eyes gleamed with both curiosity and suspicion as she studied Eva's flawless features, sensing a dangerous aura emanating from her. When she reached the group, her voice was calm, though her skin crawled with warning. "Grayson," she said, her voice laced with tension.

"Eva De Young," Grayson finally broke the silence, his words slicing through the tension like a knife. "An old...acquaintance." His voice was strained, and Raven noticed his knuckles whitening as he clenched his fists at his sides. "Eva, this is Raven Ballard."

"Pleasure to meet you," Eva purred, extending a perfectly manicured hand toward Raven. "I've heard so much about your unique bourbon tonight, Miss Ballard. It's a pleasure to make your acquaintance."

Raven hesitated, her instincts screaming at her not to take the hand but the cordiality in Eva's smile contradicting that feeling. With a reluctant nod, she accepted Eva's handshake, feeling an unfamiliar chill crawl up her arm as soon as their skin touched.

"Likewise," Raven replied cautiously, her instincts telling her to tread carefully around this mysterious woman.

As the tension in the room grew, Knox found himself torn between his duty to protect his brother and his yearning for the captivating woman who had captured both their hearts. He knew that the path ahead would be fraught with danger and heartache, but he couldn't deny the pull of destiny that seemed to entwine Grayson, Raven, and himself in its inescapable grasp.

"May I have this dance, Grayson?" Eva asked

sweetly, extending her gloved hand toward him. Her eyes sparkled with mischief, daring him to accept her offer and step into the storm once more.

With a resigned sigh, Grayson reluctantly took Eva's hand, leading her onto the dance floor as the music swelled and the world around them seemed to fade away, at least for Eva. And as Knox watched them disappear into the throng of dancers, he felt the first stirrings of that storm brewing on the horizon, one that threatened to sweep them all away in its fierce embrace.

The evening took a turn from there, with Eva skillfully weaving herself into their conversations and dances. Raven watched warily as Eva danced with Grayson, her fingers tracing circles on his broad shoulders while he maintained a respectable distance.

She felt a strange pull to intervene but held back when Knox's deep-set eyes met hers across the ballroom. He offered a reassuring smile as he approached, but it did little to quell the uneasy bubbling within her.

As the night wore on, Knox found himself gravitating toward Raven. They shared stories about their bourbon-making heritage beneath the twinkling lanterns, Knox finding comfort in their common interests and Raven appreciating his reserved nature that felt like a balm compared to Grayson's electrifying charm.

Yet even amid their shared laughter and stories, the lingering presence of Eva De Young loomed over them, a dark storm cloud threatening to cast a shadow on their newfound friendship. Raven had too many questions and Knox feared he held too many answers that could unravel the delicate peace they were just beginning to enjoy.

As the evening wound down and Eva managed to monopolize Grayson's attention again with her manipulative charm, a sense of foreboding washed over Raven. Complications were brewing much like the bourbon in the distillers all over town; slow, intoxicating, and full of critical consequences.

Eventually, Grayson found himself alone with Eva, standing out on one of many lavish balconies overlooking the pastoral landscape of Bourbon County. The scent of freshly cut grass and aging bourbon filled his nostrils, taking his mind back to simpler times before immortality had turned his life into a constant game of hide-and-seek.

"Grayson," Eva cooed, pulling him out of his thoughts. Her dark, wavy hair cascaded around her shoulders, framing her face in an alluring spectacle. "Don't you miss our old times?"

"I'm not the same person I was back then, Eva," Grayson replied coolly, his piercing blue eyes meeting hers.

The haunting melody of a slow jazz song floated through the doors of the grand manor, blending with the rhythmic hum of cicadas in the darkness. He moved them to the dance floor, to end the conversation. As the music swelled around him, Grayson danced gracefully with Eva, the weight of her presence a heavy burden on his shoulders. He glanced over at Raven, who stood near the edge of the dance floor. Raven's eyes locked onto his with an intensity that made his heart race. The pull between them was undeniable, like two magnets drawn to one another despite the distance. Grayson could see the longing in there, mirroring the emotions he tried so desperately to hide.

He turned back to Eva, who was looking at him ever so wispily, and he knew he had to get rid of her. His time with Eva should never have happened. It was a phase, but she fell in love, and he left her standing on a street in New Orleans.

"Grayson," Eva purred, drawing his attention back to her, "you seem…distracted."

"Am I?" he replied nonchalantly, his tone laced with sarcasm as he spun her around the dance floor, the music building to a crescendo.

"Ah, yes," she retorted, her amber eyes smoldering with amusement. "The famous Grayson indifference. I've missed it."

Despite his attempts to ignore her taunting, he felt the sting of her words. Eva knew him too well—or at least she thought she did. Over the years, he had learned to master the art of concealing his true feelings, only revealing what he wanted the world to see. Yet tonight, his facade was slipping beneath the weight of his conflicting emotions.

On one hand was Eva—a woman who belonged to his past, a dangerous allure that carried echoes of long-lost youth and reckless abandon. On the other was Raven—a beacon of warmth, hope, and promise, her presence sparking an unfamiliar longing in his chest.

As the music softened into a melancholic melody, Grayson led Eva in a slow dance. Their bodies moved in perfect harmony as they glided across the dance floor beneath the watchful eyes of their spectators.

His thoughts drifted back to Raven; her fiery spirit and zest for life were a stark contrast to Eva's manipulative charm. He found himself drawn to her resilience and unwavering courage—qualities he admired and yearned for.

Suddenly, Eva turned in his arms to bring herself closer to him; their bodies mere inches apart. Her voice dripped with sweetness as she whispered near his ear, "Don't think I haven't noticed your little fascination with Miss Ballard."

Grayson tensed at her words but eventually forced a smirk onto his face. "And here I thought you were losing your touch, Eva."

"Oh, never, darling," she cooed, her cool hand tracing a path up his arm, meant to be both a comfort and a warning. "We both know I have a good eye for…intrusions." Her voice was low, barely audible above the strains of jazz humming through the room.

His eyes flitted back to where he last saw Raven. She was no longer there. Instead, he found her standing by the grand fireplace, engaged in deep conversation with Knox. His brother's serious demeanor had eased into gentle smiles under Raven's animated chatter. Something close to jealousy pricked at him but he quickly quashed it down.

Grayson swallowed hard, looking again at Eva, whose amber eyes held a hint of danger. "If you're implying that Raven is an intruder, then you're mistaken. And you will bring her no harm." He spoke with a firmness that surprised even him.

She let out a throaty laughter, her breath fanning over his neck; a tempting distraction he didn't need at that moment. "Oh darling," she purred, "you underestimate me."

Over Eva's shoulder, his eyes locked onto Raven, her emerald eyes gleaming under the soft glow of the chandeliers. A pang of sympathy washed over him as he noted the brief flicker of hurt crossing her features, quickly replaced by a mask of indifference. He wondered if she was mimicking his own tactics.

The song ended, and Grayson was quick to extricate himself from Eva's clutches, his gaze returning once more to Raven across the room. "Excuse me," Grayson murmured to Eva. He gently released her hand and strode across the ballroom toward Raven, their eyes never leaving each other's. As they drew closer, the electric connection between them grew stronger, igniting the air around them with a palpable energy.

"Would you care for a dance, Miss Ballard?" Grayson asked, extending his hand to Raven.

"Of course, Mr. Beaumont," she replied, placing her delicate hand in his. Their fingers intertwined as they stepped onto the dance floor together. Their bodies moved in perfect harmony, the world around them fading into insignificance as they became lost in each other's gaze.

Knox continued to watch as they strolled away, his heart heavy with the knowledge that their intertwined destinies would bring them both joy and pain. As Grayson and Raven danced, Knox could feel the shifting winds of destiny pulling them all into each other's lives forever. The current of their interactions, the subtle glances exchanged, the silent whispers—they were all pieces of a grand puzzle yet to be revealed.

From the corner of his eye, Knox noticed Eva gliding toward him, her eyes narrowed slits of amber fury. His gut churned. Her presence was like a foul odor that permeated everything she touched.

"Knox Beaumont," she said in an overly saccharine tone. His name slipped off her tongue like a poisoned dart, aimed right at the heart. "You're not much for dancing, are you?"

He merely grunted a response, his brown eyes trained on Grayson and Raven as they danced. He saw how Grayson held her close, a tender look in his eyes that he had never seen before, not even with Eva. Raven laughed at something Grayson whispered in her ear genuine, carefree laugh that resonated around the grand ballroom.

"No," he finally replied to Eva, tearing his gaze away from them briefly. "I suppose I'm not."

"A pity," Eva continued, pouting dramatically. "This could've been our dance."

"We had our dances," Knox corrected her bluntly.

"All those years ago, it was fun for a moment," she mused with an air of nostalgia that couldn't mask her bitterness.

Knox didn't respond. Instead, he returned his attention to Raven and Grayson. He felt a pang of regret at what his brother might have to face because of his feelings for Raven. Immortals were always walking on the edge of danger and chaos—love would only complicate things. Yet looking at Grayson now, Knox couldn't bring himself to discourage him from pursuing what seemed to be true happiness.

"I see the way you look at Raven," Eva's voice broke through his musings.

He suppressed a growl at 'her insinuation. "What I feel' is none of your concern."

Eva simply lifted an eyebrow and looked back toward Grayson and Raven, who were still lost in each other. "Indeed," she murmured. "I suppose it wouldn't be."

The evening continued with an undercurrent of tension that was impossible to ignore. As the moon rose, its silver light casting long shadows across the Beaumont estate, Grayson and Raven became even more engrossed in each other, seemingly oblivious to the world around them.

Knox, however, remained vigilant. He watched Eva as she flitted around the room, her predatory gaze always returning to Grayson. He knew he couldn't let his guard down—not when so much was at stake. The weight of his responsibilities bore down on him heavily; protect the family's legacy, protect Grayson and navigate this developing fascination for Raven that was taking hold.

As the night ended, guests trickled out one by one, leaving Grayson and Raven alone on the dance floor. Knox watched as Grayson leaned down to whisper something in her ear. Whatever it made her blush, a delightful color flaming across her cheeks.

Eva stalked off into the night, leaving a trail of bitter resentment that Knox was sure would lead to future confrontations. Eventually, Knox left too, seeking solace in the quiet of his personal quarters.

As the last notes of the final song faded away, Grayson and Raven shared a lingering look, their connection growing. But both were aware that their secrets and the supernatural world they inhabited would complicate their budding friendship, casting shadows over their happiness. Each concealing their truths, not only from one another, but the world they lived in.

Chapter 3

The scent of crushed herbs and aging oak barrels greeted Grayson and Knox as they stepped into the dimly lit 'Witch's Brew' Distillery. A soft, haunting glow emanated from the brewing vats, casting shadows that danced across the walls like enchanted spirits. As their eyes adjusted to the darkness, they caught sight of Raven, her raven-black hair cascading down her back, as she carefully measured a heap of dried herbs into a gleaming copper still.

"Ah, the woman of bourbon-making herself," Grayson drawled playfully, his eyes twinkling with mischief. "I was told you were working on a new batch today."

Raven looked up, her eyes narrowing slightly as she assessed the two men before her. She smirked, the corner of her mouth lifting in a half-smile. "And what brings the Beaumont brothers to my humble abode?"

"Curiosity," Grayson replied, stepping closer as he surveyed the array of herbs spread across the wooden table. "I've heard whispers about your unique approach to crafting spirits, and I must admit, I'm intrigued."

"Whispers don't do your creations justice," Knox added, his voice low and steady as he studied the copper stills that lined the walls of the distillery. His gaze lingered on Raven for a moment, and he quickly looked away when she met his eyes.

"Is that so?" Raven asked, raising an eyebrow. Despite her sarcasm, she couldn't help but feel a flicker of pride at their interest in her work.

"Indeed," Grayson said, leaning against the table, his eyes never leaving hers. "You see, I have quite the appreciation for the art of aging spirits myself. The alchemy of turning humble grains and water into liquid gold…It's a beautiful process, isn't it?"

"Alchemy is one way to put it," Raven agreed, a hint of amusement in her voice. She gestured to the herbs on the table. "But I'm sure you know there's more to it than that. I believe that blending the right combination of herbs can not only enhance the flavor but also impart subtle magical properties to the bourbon.

"Magical properties?" Grayson asked, his curiosity on full display. He picked up a sprig of dried thyme, rubbing it between his fingers and inhaling the earthy scent.

"Oh, yes," Raven said, watching Grayson closely. "Take this thyme, for example. It's known for its purifying effects, both physically and spiritually. And when combined with other herbs, like sage and lavender, it can create a powerful elixir that promotes balance and inner peace."

"Inner peace from a glass of bourbon?" Grayson mused, a playful smirk on his lips. "I must say, that's quite the sales pitch."

"Perhaps." Raven's eyes met Grayson's, holding his gaze for a beat longer than necessary. "But some things need to be experienced to be truly understood."

"Then I look forward to experiencing it for myself," Grayson said, his voice low and charged with an intensity that sent a shiver down Raven's spine. She looked away quickly, trying to ignore the magnetic pull toward him.

"Be my quest," she replied, turning her attention back to the bottles in front of her. "Here, try this one." Handing them both a glass.

Both brothers accepted the glasses, observing the dark liquid with reserved fascination. The golden firelight from an overhead lantern reflected off its surface, casting a warm hue that made it seem as though they held tiny sunsets in their hands.

They raised the glasses to their lips, Grayson's eyes never leaving Raven's. As he took his first sip, his pupils dilated slightly. A wave of warmth flooded through him, and for a split second, he could've sworn a gentle pulse of energy radiated from the liquid. It was unlike anything he'd ever tasted—complex and earthy, with a hint of sweetness that lingered on his tongue.

Knox tasted the bourbon next, his actions slow and deliberate as always. There was a certain intensity in his gaze, an ache that he swiftly concealed behind his stoic mask. Yet, as the bourbon hit his palate and that same curious warmth spread through him, Knox found himself briefly caught off guard.

As they savored the rich, complex bourbon, both brothers couldn't help but feel a certain tingle that was entirely new. It wasn't just alcohol, there was a tranquility, a sense of balance that seemed to seep into their very bones. Raven watched them with an enigmatic smile as they shared a look between themselves before turning back to her with nods of approval.

"We're impressed," Knox admitted, his gaze

lingering on Raven longer than intended. The radiant emerald eyes, those enchanting curves emphasized by the soft glow surrounding her—it was all he could do not to reach out and brush away a stray wisp of raven-black hair from her face. "We've never tasted anything like this before."

Ignoring the tightening feeling in his chest, Grayson added, "Indeed. I dare say this spirit has a… potion of its own."

Raven's laughter filled the room, a warm and inviting sound that echoed off the stone walls. Despite their immortality and countless experiences through the century, this felt like a unique moment in time, something potent, something real. And something they were increasingly reluctant to let go of.

The amber glow of the distillery's lanterns cast a warm light over Raven's face as she meticulously measured out a handful of dried herbs. Grayson watched her with rapt attention, the scent of lavender and sage mingling with the deep aroma of aging bourbon.

"Your family has been in the business for quite some time, 'haven't they?" Grayson asked casually, leaning against a wooden barrel. "I've heard stories about the Ballard's and their…unique approach to bourbon-making."

Raven paused, her fingers hovering above the delicate mixture. She regarded him with a guarded expression, trying to gauge his intentions. "Yes, we have a long history in this town," she replied cautiously. "But I'm sure you've heard plenty of rumors about our…unconventional methods."

"Rumors, yes," Grayson conceded, his eyes

searching hers for any hint of truth. "But I find myself more interested in the truth behind them. You see, my family also has a storied past, one that is deeply intertwined with Bourbon County's heritage."

"Is that so?" Raven said, showing her curiosity despite her reservations. She resumed her work, dropping the herbs into a small cloth pouch. "And what is it that you're hoping to learn from me?"

"Perhaps we share more than just a passion for crafting spirits," Grayson suggested, his voice low and alluring. "I've always believed that there's power in understanding the past—in uncovering the secrets that bind us together."

Knox stood off to the side, silently observing the exchange between his brother and Raven. He couldn't shake the sudden pang of jealousy that stirred within him, like a dormant serpent awakened by the heat of a fire. He clenched his fists, his nails digging into his palms as he tried to suppress his emotions.

To distract himself, Knox turned his attention to the distillery's equipment, his gaze tracing the intricate network of copper pipes and valves. Bourbon-making was an art form he had always respected, and he couldn't help but admire the skill with which Raven had designed her workspace. Yet even as he studied the gleaming surfaces, his thoughts kept drifting back to the woman who stood just a few feet away.

Raven glanced between Grayson and Knox, as though aware of the tension that seemed to be building in the air. She bristled at Grayson's probing questions, as if he were attempting to peel back the layers of her carefully constructed defenses to reveal the truth hidden beneath.

"Perhaps we do share something," Raven admitted, her voice barely more than a whisper. "But some secrets are better left buried, don't you think?"

"Maybe," Grayson replied, his gaze never leaving hers. "But sometimes, there's beauty—and freedom—in embracing the truth, no matter how dark or mysterious it may be."

As their eyes locked, a shiver of anticipation ran down Raven's spine, leaving her breathless and longing for something she couldn't quite name. But as the shadows crept closer and the mysteries of their pasts threatened to consume them, she knew that the path they were walking was dangerous—a forbidden dance that could only lead to destruction.

Knox took this as his cue to leave. He could not bear to watch them flirt with one another. He moved abruptly, sending the chair he was next to scraping against the floor. All eyes swiveled toward him, including Raven's. His heart throbbed painfully in his chest, and he swore he could see a flash of something akin to disappointment in those enchanting emerald depths.

"I think I'll head home," he said tersely. His voice was steady, belying the storm of emotions roiling inside him. He met Grayson's gaze squarely, willing his brother to understand his silent plea.

Raven cleared her throat awkwardly, stepping back from the desk.' "Of course, Knox," she said softly. "Thank you for stopping by."

As he walked out, Knox didn't look back. He didn't need to see the way Grayson's eyes might linger on Raven, or how hers might respond.

Once outside, he found himself alone in the quiet

stillness of the Kentucky night. He ran a hand through his chestnut hair and took a deep breath. The scent of brewing bourbon hung heavily in the air, mixing with the earthy aroma of damp soil and the sweet scent of blooming hydrangea.

Knox turned toward the serpentine streets, stretching as far as his eyes could see. Closing his eyes and sank into the depths of his own mind... His breathing synchronized with the distant hooting of an owl and faint whispers of the wind rustling through leaves nearby.

Inside 'Witch's Brew,' Grayson watched Knox leave with a lingering sadness in his eyes. He knew his brother well enough to recognize the hurt beneath that reserved facade. But even as guilt gnawed at him, he couldn't help but be drawn further into Raven's orbit.

The soft glow of the setting sunbathed the distillery in warm hues, casting a golden light that seemed to make everything within its reach shimmer, as if enchanted. Grayson found himself captivated by the sight of Raven, her black hair cascading down her back in soft waves, as she moved with an effortless grace between the various barrels and brewing equipment that filled the room. He couldn't help but be drawn to her magnetic presence, noting the way her deep emerald eyes appeared to change in intensity as they reflected the fading sunlight.

"Here," Raven said, holding up a small vial filled with a vibrant green liquid. "This is a tincture I've been working on. It's meant to enhance the flavors of the bourbon while also providing some...unique properties."

Grayson took the vial from her hand, their fingers

brushing against each other as he did so. The brief touch sent a jolt of electricity up his arm, and he found himself momentarily lost in the depths of her gaze.

"Interesting," he murmured, raising the vial to his nose and inhaling deeply. "It smells like a blend of herbs I've never encountered before. Quite alluring."

"Much like yourself," Raven replied with a hint of a smile, her guarded exterior cracking just enough for Grayson to catch a glimpse of the woman beneath.

"Is that so?" Grayson asked, his lips curved into a playful smirk. "Perhaps we should discuss our mutual allure over a glass of this Witch's Brew. After all, it's not every day one encounters such a bewitching beauty."

Raven's cheeks flushed slightly at the compliment, though she rolled her eyes at the obvious flirtation. "You're quite the charmer, aren't you, Mr. Beaumont? But don't think your silver tongue will work its magic on me so easily."

"Ah, but you see, Miss Ballard," Grayson retorted, his blue-gray eyes sparkling with mischief, "I've always believed that the most enchanting connections are forged through a dance of wits and words. And thus far, I have to say...I'm quite enjoying our little *pas de deux*."

"Really?" Raven inquired, allowing herself a small smile as she poured two glasses of bourbon. "Well, I suppose I can't deny that there's something intriguing about this verbal sparring of ours. But be warned–I don't surrender easily."

"Neither do I," Grayson promised, clinking his glass against hers before taking a slow sip of the dark amber liquid. As the rich flavors danced across his tongue, he couldn't help but find himself more entranced by the woman before him than any concoction she could possibly create.

"Your expertise in your craft is truly remarkable," he told her sincerely, his hand brushing against hers once more as they continued their conversation. "You've breathed new life into an age-old tradition, and it's clear to me that your family's legacy is in capable hands."

"Thank you, Grayson," Raven murmured, touched by his genuine interest and respect for her work. As the sun dipped below the horizon and the shadows deepened around them, she found herself letting her guard down ever so slightly, drawn to the enigmatic man who seemed to understand her in a way few others ever had.

Yet, even as they lingered in the warm embrace of the twilight hour, lost in the intimate dance between words and stolen touches, they both knew that the secrets they harbored threatened to tear apart the fragile connection they had begun to forge. For beneath the sensual allure of their shared passion, darker forces lurked in the shadows, waiting to strike at the heart of their forbidden love.

Eva De Young's amber eyes narrowed as she watched Grayson and Raven from the shadows, her porcelain skin illuminated by the flickering glow of lanterns outside the distillery. The sight of them laughing together, their hands brushing against each other, was like a dagger to her heart. She clenched her fists, feeling the cold fury rise within her.

"Grayson," Raven said, her emerald eyes twinkling with curiosity, "tell me more about your family's history in Bourbon County. It seems our ancestors had quite the connection."

"Yes, they did," Grayson replied, his voice velvety and rich, like the bourbon he held so effortlessly between his fingers. He took a measured sip before continuing. "The Beaumont's have been here since the early days of Bourbon County, building their fortune on the land's magic and the spirits it produced."

Raven leaned in closer, captivated by his words and the intensity of his gaze. "I've always sensed something…unique about the Beaumont estate. I never realized your roots ran so deep."

"Ah, but it's not just our roots," Grayson murmured, moving closer still, his breath warm against her cheek. "It's the way it mingles with yours, the way our families have been intertwined for generations."

As Grayson's words hung in the air, charged with an unmistakable electricity, Eva bristled with jealousy. How dare this woman bewitch him so completely, stealing his attention and affection? Grayson belonged to her–or at least, he would soon enough.

With a predatory grace, Eva slipped away from the window, her mind racing with plans to win Grayson back and eliminate the competition that stood in her way. A wicked smile played across her lips as she imagined the delicious torment she would unleash upon Raven Ballard, ensuring that she would never come between her and Grayson again.

Unaware of the danger lurking in the shadows, Grayson continued to share stories of his family's history, weaving a tapestry of love, loss, and ambition that spoke to the heart of Bourbon County. As he spoke, the weight of his past seemed to lift from his shoulders, replaced by an undeniable connection to the woman beside him.

"Raven," he whispered, tracing the curve of her jaw with the back of his hand, "I feel like I've known you for centuries, like our destinies have been intertwined since the beginning."

"Grayson," she breathed, her voice husky, while her eyes were locked with his. "It's too much, too soon. We can't—"

"Shh," he silenced her gently, his thumb brushing against her lower lip. "I know. But the pull between us...it's impossible to ignore."

For a heartbeat, they stood there, lost in each other's electrostatic presence, the secrets they harbored threatening to tear them apart even as their desire threatened to consume them. And all the while, Eva De Young plotted in the darkness, her jealousy and obsession growing ever more powerful, setting the stage for a deadly game of love and betrayal.

****

The warm glow of twilight bathed the Beaumont estate in a golden haze, casting long shadows that danced across the verdant landscape. Knox stood at the edge of the Beaumont distillery, his deep brown eyes watching Grayson return, along with Raven by his side, a mixture of admiration and envy running through him. His chestnut hair rustled softly in the breeze as he turned away, trying to focus on the task at hand.

"Are you all right, Knox?" Grayson asked, concern lacing his tone as he caught his brother's gaze.

"Of course," Knox replied, forcing a smile. "I'm just...preoccupied with perfecting our new bourbon blend." As he spoke, he couldn't help but steal another glance at Raven, her lithe figure framed by the setting sun.

"Ah, I understand," Grayson answered, his voice tinged with amusement. "Well, don't let us distract you from your work."

As Grayson returned his attention to Raven, Knox found solace in the meticulous art of the task at hand. The comforting scent of aging spirits filled the air as he carefully measured and mixed ingredients, using his immortal senses to discern the most subtle of flavors.

"Knox," Grayson called out, breaking his concentration. "Why don't you join us for a walk around the estate? The moon is full tonight, and the grounds are particularly captivating."

"Thank you, Grayson, but I have much work to do here," Knox replied, his heart aching at the thought of spending more time near Raven, knowing she was slipping further out of reach.

"Suit yourself," Grayson said, an impish grin playing on his lips. He turned to Raven, his blue-gray eyes darkening with desire. "Shall we?"

"Lead the way," Raven replied, her eyes sparkling seductively.

As the pair wandered away from the distillery on the south side of the estate, Knox's thoughts were consumed by a whirlwind of emotions. Loyalty to his brother was awakened with his burgeoning feelings for Raven, leaving him torn and confused. He poured his frustrations into his work, focusing on the delicate balance of flavors in his bourbon blend.

Meanwhile, Grayson and Raven strolled through the estate's moonlit paths, the silvery light casting a dreamlike glow on their surroundings. Their conversation flowed easily, touching on their deepest dreams and fears as they wandered beneath the ancient trees.

"Sometimes, I feel like I'm trapped in this existence," Grayson confessed, his voice tinged with melancholy. "I long for the simple pleasures of life, but they're always just out of reach."

"Grayson," Raven murmured, her tone laced with empathy, "being who we are…it's not easy, I am sure. But we have the power to change the world around us, to shape our own destinies. It's a gift."

"Maybe you're right," Grayson agreed, his gaze locked with hers.

As the pair continued to share their innermost thoughts, the boundaries between them began to blur, their connection growing stronger under the moon's watchful gaze. In that moment, the walls they both had placed around them seem to have fallen away, replaced by the undeniable pull between them—an irresistible force that threatened to consume them both.

The scents of summer seemed to surround them, mingling with the subtle whispers of a warm breeze. Moonlight illuminated the intricate ironwork of the estate's gates, casting shadows upon the gravel paths that meandered through the lush gardens.

"Grayson," Raven breathed, her voice low with the rustle of leaves and the distant song of cicadas. "It's beautiful out here."

"Wait until you see the rose garden," he replied, a hint of mischief playing at the corners of his lips. He led her by the hand, their fingers interlaced as they navigated the moonlit paths together.

Meanwhile, hidden within the shadows, Eva De

Young watched the pair with growing unease. Her obsidian gaze narrowed, her eyes flickering like embers as she began to formulate a plan. It was time to gather information about Raven's weaknesses and vulnerabilities, using them to manipulate Grayson and drive a wedge between him and this woman.

"Tell me, Raven," Grayson asked, his voice low and tender as they reached the heart of the fragrant rose garden, "what are your dreams? What do you truly desire?"

Raven hesitated for a moment before confiding in him. "I want to continue my family's legacy, honoring their wisdom while forging my own path. But more than anything, I crave a happy normal life, one where I am free."

Grayson looked into her eyes, seeing the vulnerability and longing that lay beneath the surface. Her courage and strength captivated him, drawn to her in ways he couldn't quite comprehend.

"Raven," he whispered, his breath warm against her skin as he leaned in closer, "I think we may share some of the same thoughts."

Their lips met in a passionate kiss, a union of fire and ice that set their very souls alight. It was as if the universe itself conspired to bring them together, weaving a tapestry of desire and longing that threatened to consume them both.

Eva's heart twisted and churned in the shadows, consumed by a seething mix of jealousy and rage. She made a dark vow to herself, promising to use every weapon at her disposal to rip apart Grayson and Raven's relationship, no matter what the sacrifices.

"Grayson is mine," she hissed venomously through

gritted teeth, her eyes blazing with malevolent intent. "And I will not allow this woman to steal him away from me."

In that moment, the lines were drawn, and the stage was set for a battle of hearts—one that would test the bonds between Grayson, Knox, and Raven, and ultimately reveal the true depths of Eva's dark, vampiric nature.

The moon hung low and heavy in the sky, casting a silvery glow across the lush gardens of the Beaumont estate. Grayson's hands found their way to Raven's waist as they stood on the bridge overlooking the wild beauty of the rushing stream below. The sound of water seemed to mirror the intensity of their emotions, creating an atmosphere both exhilarating and dangerous.

"Grayson," Raven breathed, her voice a soft whisper above the symphony of nature around them. "What are we doing? This is madness."

"Perhaps," he murmured, his eyes never leaving hers. "But isn't there something thrilling about dancing on the edge of the abyss, knowing that one misstep could send us spiraling into the unknown?"

Raven's breath caught in her throat as she considered his words. She knew the risks—the strict taboo against dating and someone finding out her truth, the potential consequences should her secret be discovered, but the fire that ignited within her when she was near him was impossible to resist.

"Maybe," she admitted, a smile tilting the corners of her lips. "But it's a dangerous game we're playing, Grayson. One I'm not sure I can win."

"Then let's not worry about the rules," he

suggested, his fingers tracing patterns along her skin, sending shivers down her spine. "Together, we can forge new rules, ones that defy reason, transcending boundaries and expectations."

"Is such a thing even possible?" she asked, her gaze locked onto his, searching for answers in the depths of his blue-gray eyes.

"Anything is possible," he replied, his voice low and full of conviction. "If we dare to believe in the impossible."

As Grayson and Raven continued their intimate conversation, Eva watched from behind a curtain of ivy, her heart aching with rage. She clutched a small vial of blood in her hand, its crimson contents swirling ominously.

"Grayson," she whispered, her eyes narrowing as she took in the sight of him with Raven, the object of her obsession slipping further from her grasp. "I'll make you understand."

With a determined glint in her eyes, Eva turned away from the scene before her and disappeared into the shadows. Her mind raced with cruel intentions, with the blood of an unknown entity coursing through her veins. Eva was more than a jealous lover. She transformed into the embodiment of a dangerous obsession, and she wouldn't stop until Grayson was hers once again.

Suddenly, a chilling wind whipped through the grove. The leaves rustled loudly, and a black raven landed on a branch nearby. It cawed ominously before taking flight again. Raven watched it disappear against the darkening sky with a sense of foreboding.

And so, it started–a twisted dance of secrets and

desires, a dangerous game where hearts were the chips on the table. Little did they know this dance would have far-reaching consequences not just for them, but for the delicate balance between their worlds. Bourbon County was about to become a battleground of love, power, and betrayal, where only the strongest hearts would survive.

As Grayson held Raven close, neither of them could have guessed what was going down. All they knew was this moment, one they both knew, could destroy them. But for now, they allowed themselves to be swept up in the current of their blossoming passion, surrendering to the intoxicating allure of forbidden love that hung heavy in the air like the scent of roses and secrets waiting to be revealed.

Chapter 4

As the sun dipped below the horizon, casting the sky in a kaleidoscope of fiery oranges and deep purples, Grayson led Raven through the ancient oak trees that stood sentinel over the Beaumont estate. Faint notes of jazz drifting from the main house created a tranquil atmosphere.

"Where are we going?" Raven asked, her eyes sparkling with curiosity as she tried to decipher Grayson's intentions.

"Patience, my dear," he replied, his voice smooth like honey. "I promise it'll be worth the wait."

They emerged into a secluded clearing, where a canopy of twinkling fairy lights illuminated an intimate table draped in white linen. A gentle breeze rustled the leaves above them, carrying with it the soft murmur of a nearby stream.

"Grayson, this is beautiful," Raven breathed, awestruck by the romantic scene before her.

"Only the best for you," he whispered, pulling out her chair with a flourish.

As they settled into their seats, the playful banter between them flowed as easily as the aged bourbon they sipped. Their laughter filled the night air, each witty retort and teasing comment drawing them closer together. With every lingering glance, the electricity between them intensified, until the space between their entwined fingers seemed charged with possibility.

Grayson's voice dripped with desire as he whispered to Raven, "Do you want to explore the rest of the estate?" His invitation hung in the air, heavy and loaded with implication.

Raven's heart raced as she nodded, knowing that there was no turning back.

As Grayson led Raven up the grand staircase, their bodies pressed close together, their hands intertwined with an urgency that was palpable. The moonlight poured through the windows, casting a soft, ethereal glow on the antique furniture in Grayson's bedroom.

With a low growl, Grayson pulled Raven into his arms, his lips crashing down onto hers with a passion that left her breathless. He nipped at her bottom lip, his tongue darting out to taste her sweetness. Raven moaned softly, her hands running up his chest and into his hair.

Grayson's hands roamed over 'her body', exploring every curve and contour. He cupped her breasts, his thumbs flicking over her hard nipples. Raven gasped, her body trembling with desire.

With deft fingers, Grayson unzipped her dress, letting it pool at her feet. He stepped back to admire her, his eyes dark with lust. Raven stood before him in nothing but her lacy underwear, her body on display for his hungry gaze.

Grayson hooked his thumbs into the waistband of her panties and slowly slid them down her legs. He kneeled before her, pressing a kiss on her inner thigh. Raven's legs trembled as Grayson's lips moved higher, his tongue darting out to taste her wetness.

Raven's fingers tangled in Grayson's hair as he

pleasured her, his tongue working wonders between her legs. She moaned his name, her body responding to his touch with an intensity that was almost overwhelming.

When Grayson finally stood, Raven could see the bulge in his pants, straining against the fabric. She reached for him, her fingers curling around his hard length. Grayson groaned, his hips bucking involuntarily.

With a growl, Grayson pulled Raven onto the bed, their bodies tangled together. He kissed her deeply, their tongues dancing together as their hands explored each other's bodies. Raven could feel the heat building between them, her body aching for release.

He reached between them, guiding himself inside her. Raven gasped at the sensation, her body stretching to accommodate him. He moved, thrusting slowly at first and then with increasing speed. Raven's nails dug into his back as she met him thrust for thrust, their bodies moving in perfect rhythm.

Grayson's lips found hers again, their kisses deep and passionate. Raven could feel herself getting closer and closer to the edge, her body trembling with desire. With a final, powerful thrust, Grayson sent her over the edge, her body convulsing with pleasure.

They lay together, their bodies slick with sweat and their hearts racing. Grayson pressed a kiss to Raven's forehead, his arms wrapping around her tightly. She snuggled into his embrace, her body still humming with pleasure.

As they lay there, basking in the afterglow, Raven couldn't help but think that this was the most romantic experience of her life. Grayson had made her feel desired and loved, and she'd never forget this night.

****

The morning light spilled through the gauzy curtains, casting dancing light on the tangled sheets and exposed skin. Raven stirred, her eyes fluttering open as she took in the sight of Grayson's chiseled jawline and tousled jet-black hair. For a fleeting moment, she relished the warmth of his body pressed against hers, the steady rhythm of his breathing lulling her into a sense of security.

With a reluctant sigh, she carefully untangled herself from 'his embrace, pulling on her clothes with quiet haste. Her heart raced as she tiptoed across the room, pausing at the door to steal one last glance at the man who had captivated her so completely. But even as she stepped into the hallway, she couldn't shake the feeling that their stolen night of passion would come at a price.

No sooner had she closed the bedroom door behind her than Eva De Young appeared at the end of the corridor, her porcelain skin and dark, wavy hair making her seem like a specter from another era. A predatory smile played on her lips as she sauntered toward Raven, her amber eyes gleaming with mischief.

"Leaving so soon, darling?" Eva purred, her voice dripping with false sweetness. "I do hope you enjoyed your evening with Grayson."

Raven stiffened, her instincts screaming at her to flee from the dangerous woman before her. But with a defiant tilt of her chin, she held her ground. "That's none of your business."

"Ah, but it is," Eva countered, her tone shifting from sultry to sinister. "You see, I've discovered something quite...interesting about you, dear Raven."

She paused for dramatic effect, letting her words hang heavy in the air. "You're a witch, aren't you?"

Raven's blood ran cold, and for a moment, she was rendered speechless. How could Eva possibly know her deepest secret? Before she could respond, the sound of a door creaking open startled them both.

"Raven?" Grayson's voice, groggy from sleep, echoed through the hallway as he emerged from his room. His gaze darted between the two women, confusion etched on his handsome face. "What's going on?"

"Ask your little friend here," Eva spat, her gaze locked on Raven with venomous intensity. "It seems she's been hiding quite a bit from you, Grayson."

Raven could only stare back at Eva, a thousand words frozen in her throat. She could feel Grayson's eyes on her, confusion shifting to concern.

"Raven?" His voice was deeper now, no longer muddled with sleep. Wearily, she turned to meet his gaze; the pain and betrayal reflected there were like a knife to her heart.

"I—" Her voice cracked under the weight of her secret. All she could manage in the moment was, "I have to go." With those words Raven ran from the house, devastated, confused and scared her secret was out. Reaching the car, her tears spilled out, making it difficult to drive the few miles to her distillery and her friends.

Raven drove aimlessly through the verdant hills of Bourbon County, her mind a whirlwind of thoughts and emotions. The atmosphere in the car was thick with her tears, creating a bleak symphony of sorrow that reverberated through the aging vehicle.

Finally, she found herself outside 'Witch's Brew' where Marley and Madison were working today to cover for Raven. She barely had time to go into the door when she saw Marley's concerned face.

"Raven?" she questioned worriedly, "What happened?" You look like you've seen a ghost."

"I..." Raven began, but her voice trailed off as tears threatened to spill. Madison joined them at the doorway, her face mirroring Marley's concern.

"Come into the office," Madison offered gently, standing aside to allow Raven some room to move.

Once settled on the worn-out couch in Raven's office with a cup of chamomile tea steaming between her hands, Raven began recounting the morning's events. Every word she spoke seemed like pouring salt on an open wound. She could see shock and concern etch themselves onto her friends' faces as they grappled with the reality of what she revealed.

"Eva, the woman we saw with Grayson and Knox at the party, knows I'm a witch," she concluded dejectedly. "And now Grayson does too, I am sure."

Marley and Madison shared a glance that held volumes. The silence stretched out between them until finally Marley broke it.

"What are we going to do?" Her voice was so shaky; fear laced each syllable. It was a question none of them knew the answer to.

****

Meanwhile, back at the Beaumont estate, Grayson paced restlessly in his room. Until he was ready to hear what Eva had to say. Dressing quickly, he headed down the stairs to the den where Eva sat. Smily like a cat that just caught a mouse.

"Speak," he commanded, his voice cold and distant. Eva's smile faltered slightly, but she recovered quickly, rising languidly from the plush leather chair.

"Oh, Grayson," she cooed. "You never did like to be kept in the dark, did you?" She circled him slowly, like a vulture stalking its wounded prey.

"Out with it, Eva," he snapped impatiently, his chiseled features drawn tight with tension.

"All right," she conceded, tilting her head coyly. "Your little Raven is a witch. Can you imagine?" Her laughter echoed around the room, a discordant melody that set his teeth on edge.

The words hit him like a punch to the gut. "What?"

"Yes! Seems you've been sleeping with the enemy." Her triumphant smile turned cruel. "Forbidden fruit has always been your weakness."

His heart pounded in his chest at the word. Witch. The word felt like acid in his mouth. Yet somewhere deep inside his chaotic mind was a tiny voice that whispered—it all makes sense now.

"And why should I believe you?" he spat out; his tone icy.

Eva smirked, revealing her white teeth. "Why would I lie? Especially about something so…dangerous," she said, dragging out the last word for effect.

He remained silent as Eva's words washed over him. The pill was bitter to swallow—betrayal sliced through him like a scorching blade. Raven, a witch? The realization felt surreal, impossible even.

"Doubt all you want." Eva's voice dripped venom as she continued her lurid revelations. "But it's true."

Grayson sank into the chair Eva had vacated, his

mind whirling with disjointed thoughts and emotions. *A witch...Raven is a witch...*the thought kept repeating in his head like an unending loop.

The mansion felt suffocating in its luxuriousness, the silence pressing against him with the weight of a century of secrets and lies. Grayson stared aimlessly at the high ceiling. The intricately carved rosewood panels that adorned them, once admired for their beauty, now felt cold and mocking.

Eva let out a victorious chuckle, her eyes gleaming with malice as she watched him crumble under the revelation. She moved to stand behind him, her fingers grazing his shoulder, but he shrugged her off.

"Don't touch me," he muttered through gritted teeth, clenching his hands into tight fists. Eva recoiled slightly but held her ground.

"Grayson..." she began in a tone bordering on gentleness. He turned to face her then, his expression hardened with anger and betrayal. Eyes blazing red, his true nature that was usually locked up tight shown true.

"I said DON'T!" He snarled, rising abruptly from his seat, causing Eva to step back, taken aback by the ferocity of his words.

A knock on the door interrupted their tense standoff. Knox stepped into the room, his face drawn into a tight mask of worry as he took in the palpable tension between Grayson and Eva.

"I heard shouting...what happened?" His tone was guarded as he glanced from Grayson to Eva, an unspoken question hanging in the air between them.

"It seems your' little Raven has been keeping secrets," Eva cooed from behind him, her amber eyes glinting in perverse satisfaction as she turned her gaze upon Knox.

"What are you on about, Eva?" Knox sneered, casting her a dismissive glare before focusing back on Grayson. However, Grayson remained silent, lost in his turmoil.

With a triumphant smirk, Eva repeated her revelation. Yet again, the single word sent shockwaves through the room. "Witch."

The silence that followed was nearly suffocating. Even Eva seemed taken aback by Knox's lack of response. His expression remained unreadable as he moved to Grayson's side and turned to face Eva.

"You seem rather pleased with yourself," Knox's voice was ice cold as he studied Eva. "But your petty attempts at mischief won't work here."

"I merely revealed the truth." Her voice was syrupy sweet yet held an edge of malice as she responded.

As if suddenly tired of the conversation, Knox turned back to Grayson, whose eyes were still filled with disbelief and confusion.

"Go check on Raven," he suggested gently, his tone softer now as he addressed his brother. "Talk to her…see her side of the story."

Though still shaken by the revelation, Grayson nodded slowly. Standing up with a newfound determination reflecting in his eyes, he left to find Raven without sparing Eva another glance.

Once Grayson had left, Knox turned back to Eva, his ice-cold eyes hard as he regarded her. "You best remember your place, Eva De Young." His voice was a low growl. "I won't tolerate any more of these games."

With that menacing warning hanging in the air, Knox followed his brother's steps out of the room, leaving a stunned Eva behind.

****

Back at Witch's Brew distillery, Raven was in turmoil. Madison had suggested reaching out to the Witch's Council for help, but Raven knew better than to involve the council; they wouldn't understand. They would say she never protected the secret.

"No," she said firmly. "I won't go to them." Marley and Madison exchanged glances but didn't question her decision.

As Raven grappled with her fear and uncertainty in the refuge of her distillery, Grayson was wrestling with a revelation of his own.

The car felt suffocating, the air heavy with unspoken truths and forbidden desires. Grayson downed in his emotions. He had to find Raven, confront her, seek answers for this sudden whirlwind they were both unwillingly thrown into.

As the night fell on the county, its silent fields echoed with secrets. Lost in their own worlds, Grayson and Raven were adrift in a sea of revelations and betrayals, their hearts yearning for each other amidst the storm.

Knox had retreated to his dimly lit office, his sanctuary amidst the chaos that had erupted in the Beaumont estate. The scent of aging bourbon and damp earth filled the air, enveloping him in a comforting embrace as he focused on his work, a new bourbon blend that demanded his full attention.

His hands moved with practiced precision, measuring and mixing ingredients with an almost obsessive care. Each drop of liquid was a testament to his dedication to his craft, a silent plea for solace from the storm of emotions raging within him. His attraction to Raven was a secret burden, and now her newly revealed witch heritage only added more layers of complexity to his already tumultuous feelings.

As Knox meticulously poured the amber liquid from an oak barrel, his mind drifted back to the confrontation between Grayson and Eva earlier. He could still hear the tense exchanges, the pain in Grayson's voice when confronted with the truth, and the shock and confusion of it all was tearing his brother apart.

And for his own part? Knox couldn't deny the surprise that had seized him as he heard the truth about Raven, his fingers pausing over the delicate glass vial. A witch. The whispers of old tales from their childhood filled his mind, stories of powerful women who could commune with the earth and read the patterns in the stars. And to think that Raven herself was one of such women–it was an astonishing realization.

Knox shook his head, trying to focus on the task at hand. Yet the image of Raven's emerald eyes filled with unshed tears haunted him. He recalled her quiet strength, her fierce independence that had captivated him from their first meeting at that lavish summer party amidst the entire county. What he had dismissed as intelligence and charm was perhaps something more profound connection borne from their shared love for this land, a connection now tinged with hints of mysticism.

****

Back at Witch's Brew distillery, Raven continued her struggle against the rising tide of fear and uncertainty gnawing at her sanity. She moved around aimlessly, her thoughts consumed by Grayson's shattered gaze as he came to know of her heritage.

Marley's reassuring hand on Raven's shoulder pulled her out of her reverie. "We'll figure this out, Rae," her voice was gentle but firm, a steady rock amidst the tempest that threatened to swallow them all.

Raven nodded, attempting a weak smile of gratitude. Her friends were her lifeline now—beacons in the darkness of her despair and confusion. They had encouraged her to shower and drink more tea to calm her. It was helping, but she was still anxious. Making her pace all around the office, hoping he would understand why she never told him.

****

Grayson pulled up outside Raven's distillery in his sleek black car, the engine rumbling quietly under the soft glow of the moonlight. He took a deep breath before stepping out, steeling himself for the confrontation ahead. His mind was a whirlwind of emotions—anger, confusion, betrayal—all tangled up in an unsettling dread. But deep down, he knew he had kept secrets of his own. If he had known hers, then he could have shared his.

A brooding intensity replaced his usually charming demeanor as he approached the distillery. His heart pounded in his chest, matching the rhythm of his doubts. The sight of Raven's shadow moving restlessly behind the windows further fueled his anxiety.

Finally gathering courage, he pushed open the door to face Raven, ready to uncover their shared truths and put an end to the secrets that threatened to tear them apart. The faint smell of chamomile tea hit him as he stepped into the softly lit room, and for a moment, he stood caught in the bittersweet familiarity of it all.

Raven paled as she took in Grayson's tense figure. He felt her tension. He could see her brace herself for the torrent of emotions about to be unleashed. He sensed all these emotions at once making him realize how unstable he was in the moment.

As their eyes met amidst the dim light and soft shadows of the distillery, they both knew that tonight would change everything, revealing a world intertwined with forbidden love, concealed truths, and unspoken desires. Grayson knew at that moment, he had to confess his own hidden world, for if she already knew, and she played him, it would all be over before it ever began.

The air between them crackled with tension, a tangible force that caused every breath to feel ragged, every heartbeat erratic. The silence was suffocating, only the ticking of an old wrought iron clock hanging on the distillery's stone wall echoing throughout the room.

Finally, Grayson broke the silence, his voice barely rising above a whisper. "Why didn't you tell me?" His eyes bored into hers, a whirlpool of emotions concealed within. "You should've told me about your...about your witch heritage."

Raven swallowed hard, her throat tight with unshed tears. "I wanted to," she confessed, her voice trembling slightly. "But you must understand...it's forbidden. For witches to tell anyone except family or those sworn to uphold the secret." She fell silent at his sharp breath.

He moved closer, the sound of his boots echoing ominously against the wooden floor. He looked at her, studying her face, searching for any signs of deceit. She returned his gaze unflinchingly, her eyes shining bright in the semi-darkness. Her lips were a firm line, her chin held high–a silent challenge.

"Raven," Grayson began, his voice rough and low, "I was so upset, and confused."

His words hung heavily in the room as he waited for her response. Raven looked anxiously at Marley and Madison, who stood by the doorway like silent sentinels. She knew she had to be brave now–not just for herself, but for all witches of Bourbon County who were under threat of exposure.

He reached out to touch her but hesitated midway and let his hand drop to his side. His fingers flexed nervously as he gathered his thoughts.

"I'm so sorry about my behavior earlier," he started softly. "I was out of line." His gaze lowered on the floorboards.

An awkward silence filled the room as he stumbled over his words to express what he was feeling, something he'd never had a problem with before. But this wasn't an ordinary situation, and Raven wasn't just any woman.

"Raven," he began, and his voice was rough with strain. "There is…there is something else you need to know about me."

Raven sucked in a sharp breath, her eyes widening. She had begged for honesty, but now that it was here, the prospect of yet another revelation terrified her. She leaned into his touch regardless, prompting him silently to continue.

"I'm not…I'm not exactly human either," he confessed, his words tumbling out in a rush as if he feared she'd disappear if he took too long to say them.

Her heart skipped a beat. Not exactly human? What did that mean? Could Grayson be like her? A witch? But then she remembered stories from her grandparents about the vampires in Bourbon County a century ago.

"Grayson," she whispered, her voice trembling, "are you a vampire?" As she spoke the words, she heard her friends gasp and felt the vibes in the room change.

She watched as he drew in a deep breath, stealing himself before speaking slowly. "Not exactly, I am an Immortal. Same family you could say, different level."

The words hung heavily in the air between them, a confirmation of their shared secret worlds. A world where witches fell for immortals and they fell for witches; where secrets intertwined with desires, where any love of this kind would be forbidden, but relentless, nonetheless.

Raven took a step back, trying to process this new information. A sense of relief washed over her. He wasn't just a mortal who'd been manipulated or deceived into loving a witch; he was someone who understood what it meant to carry an extraordinary secret while appearing ordinary. Being from the supernatural world meant she had not broken the rule of an ordinary human finding out. But this relief was short-lived as another realization hit her—their relationship stood against every rule set by the Witch's Council. The punishment, if discovered, would be severe. Raven glanced at her friends, searching for their thoughts.

Marley and Madison's expressions mirrored her own. Fear, relief, and shock were reflected in their wide eyes, their lips pressed into thin lines. Things had escalated beyond anyone's control, beyond anyone's understanding.

"Raven," Marley finally spoke, breaking the uneasy silence that had descended upon the room. Her voice was soft, sympathetic, but laced with worry. "This changes everything."

The gravity of her words hung heavily in the air, the implications echoing in the silence that followed. As if on cue, a soft sound filled the distillery—it was the wind howling outside, whistling through the old wooden walls. The world outside felt distant and threatening, as though sensing the uproar within.

Grayson sighed heavily, raking a hand through his tousled black hair. His stormy eyes reflected a desperate need for understanding, for acceptance. "I'm sorry," he began again, looking at Raven with a mix of regret and determination. "I never meant to complicate things."

Raven swallowed hard, summoning all her strength to meet his gaze. "And yet here we are," she replied quietly, her heart pounding in her chest.

She knew then that there was no turning back now. Their secrets were revealed, exposing their forbidden worlds and hidden lives.

Grayson stepped closer to her again, his piercing gaze never leaving hers. He spoke in a whisper as he said, "Raven...I cannot change what I am nor do away with my feelings for you." His voice held a note of desperation but also resilience. "We may be forbidden by laws and rules set by others...but what we feel for each other...Isn't it worth fighting for?"

The electricity between them heightened at his words. Raven looked up at him, her heart in knots as she whispered back with raw honesty dripping from every word, "Yes…"

"Then we'll fight together," Grayson said fiercely, his jaw set in determination.

"Is that really an option?" Raven questioned, her heart aching at the thought of turning against her own kind. "This isn't just about us, Grayson. It's about preserving the balance between our worlds. If we defy the counsel, we could plunge everything into chaos."

"Maybe it's time for change," Grayson countered, taking a step toward her. "Why should we let ancient laws dictate our lives?"

"Grayson, you don't understand," Raven said, shaking her head. "We're playing with fire. The magic that binds witches and immortals is powerful and unpredictable. Our love could ignite a war between our people."

"Isn't it worth fighting for?" Grayson asked, his voice barely whispered as he reached out to gently touch her cheek.

"Grayson…" Raven's heart yearned to give in to the passion that coursed through her veins like wildfire. But deep down, she knew that surrendering to their desires could bring about destruction beyond anything they could imagine.

"Raven," Grayson murmured, his fingers brushing over her lips as if trying to memorize every curve and contour. "Tell me you don't feel the same way."

"I do," she admitted, her voice cracking under the weight of her confession. "But sometimes, such feelings aren't enough."

As Grayson's hand slipped away from her face, Raven felt an icy coldness settle in her chest. A part of her longed to throw caution to the wind and follow her heart, but another part understood the gravity of her situation. She was torn between her duty as a witch and her desire for Grayson, with no clear path forward.

"Then we'll find another way," Grayson said, his eyes filled with a fierce determination that both terrified and thrilled her.

"Will we really?" Her voice filled with doubt. "Or are we just delaying the inevitable?"

"Maybe," Grayson replied, his voice heavy with emotion. "But I can't let you go without a fight, Raven. I won't."

"Grayson…" Raven whispered, her heart swelling with a mixture of hope and fear. As she stared into his stormy eyes, she knew that no matter what they chose, their lives would never be the same again. And as the darkness closed in around them, the only certainty was that their friendship had set them on a collision course with destiny—one that threatened to consume them both in its fiery embrace.

Meanwhile, Knox kept pacing the floor of his study, images of Raven haunting his every step. He knew he should respect his brother's relationship, but the intensity of his feelings for her made it nearly impossible. As he poured himself a glass of bourbon, he tried to drown the longing that threatened to consume him.

"Dammit," he muttered, slamming the glass onto the table. "Why did it have to be her?"

He couldn't shake the image of Raven's heartbreaking eyes, filled with a tender warmth that stirred something within him he couldn't quite name. His heart raced as he recalled the stolen moments they'd shared, the lingering touches that seemed to promise more.

"Knox?" Wixx's voice broke through his reverie, his expression etched with concern. "Is everything all right?"

"Fine," Knox lied, placing the empty glass back on the table. "Just...thinking."

"About Raven?" Wixx asked, his eyes narrowing with suspicion. Wixx misses nothing.

"Of course not," Knox snapped, immediately regretting his harsh tone. "I just...have a lot on my mind."

"Right," Wixx said, clearly unconvinced. "Well, if you ever need to talk, I'm here."

"Thanks," Knox replied, forcing a smile. He watched as Wixx left the room, his heart heavy with the weight of secrets and unspoken desires.

As the night wore on, the air grew thick with tension, both brothers caught in an emotional storm they could not escape. Eva's games had set events into motion, her dark intentions taking over their once peaceful lives. And now, with the truth of Raven's witch heritage exposed, and their own immortality, the stakes were higher than ever before.

For Grayson and Knox, the battle for love was only just beginning—and the price of victory might be more than they could ever imagine.

****

Days later, after the dust started to settle, the sun dipped low on the horizon, casting a warm golden hue across the Beaumont estate as Grayson and Raven stood at the edge of the sprawling property. The scent of fresh cut bluegrass mixed with wildflowers in full bloom mixed, creating an intoxicating blend that seemed to echo the intensity of their newfound connection.

"Grayson," Raven whispered, her eyes locked onto his, "we need to prepare for what's coming."

He nodded solemnly, fully aware of the dangers they now faced. Eva would stop at nothing to tear them apart and claim him for herself, and the Witch's Council loomed like a dark cloud over their forbidden relationship.

"Raven, I promise you, we'll face whatever obstacles come," Grayson said firmly, his hand clasping hers tightly. "Together, we got this." His smile widened, making Raven laugh.

"Even the wrath of the Witch's Council?" she asked, her voice wavering with fear.

"Especially their wrath," he replied confidently.

As the last light of day faded, Grayson and Raven were bathed in the eerie glow of the moon, their shadows stretching out before them like omens of the trials ahead. They knew that the path they had chosen was fraught with danger–not only from Eva and the supernatural world, but also from within themselves.

"Tomorrow, we'll gather our allies and devise a plan," Grayson declared, determination etched across his handsome features.

"Marley and Madison will stand by us. We'll consult with Wixx, too," Raven added, grateful for the unwavering support of her friends and the wise counsel of the Grayson's family member.

"Knox…" Grayson hesitated, conflicted emotions simmering just beneath the surface. He knew his brother struggled with hidden feelings for Raven, though he thought Grayson did not know, and the tension between them threatened to undermine their bond.

"We'll deal with Knox together," Raven assured him, sensing his turmoil. "He's your family, Grayson. We'll help him understand that we need him too."

As they stood hand in hand in the abyss of an uncertain future, Grayson and Raven steeled themselves for the battles to come. They knew that the road ahead would test the limits of their relationship and loyalty– but with each other by their side, they were prepared to face it head-on.

"Until the end of time," Grayson whispered, as he pulled Raven into a tender embrace.

"Until the end of time," she agreed, her voice filled with conviction and what felt like love.

Their moment of quiet strength was interrupted by the distant sound of hooves pounding against the earth– a harbinger of the challenges and heartache that lay in wait. As they turned toward the approaching storm, Grayson and Raven knew their journey had only just begun, and the darkness that lurked on the horizon would test them in ways they could never have imagined. But they also knew that love, like the strongest of magic, was a force to be reckoned with– and together, they would fight for their destiny with every breath in their bodies.

Chapter 5

The moon cast a silvery glow over the Beaumont estate, illuminating the lush Kentucky grass and casting eerie shadows on the centuries-old manor house. Inside, Grayson and Knox stood in the dimly lit drawing-room, their conversation growing increasingly tense as they spoke in hushed tones.

"Gray, we need to be more careful," cautioned Knox, running a hand through his tousled hair. "Our plan for the bourbon hinges on secrecy, and Eva's obsession with you is only going to draw unwanted attention."

Grayson paced the room like a caged animal, his jaw clenched as he thought of the sultry, manipulative vampire who had been haunting every step since his return to Bourbon County. "I know, Knox, I know," he responded irritably. "But it's not like I invited her into my life. She's cunning and relentless. She won't stop until she gets what she wants."

Knox regarded his brother thoughtfully, his deep brown eyes filled with concern. "Then we must be even more relentless in protecting our family legacy, and each other." He paused, clearly weighing his words carefully before continuing. "Perhaps it's time we took...drastic measures."

As Grayson opened his mouth to respond, the heavy oak doors of the drawing room burst open with a bang. A rush of chilly air swept through the room, carrying with it the intoxicating scent of roses and nightshade. Eva De Young stood in the doorway, her porcelain skin glowing ethereally beneath the soft moonlight that streamed through the windows. Her eyes focused solely on Grayson, while her dark, wavy hair framed her face like a halo of shadows.

"Grayson," she purred, her voice dripping with seductive charm. "It seems I've interrupted quite the little tête-à-tête. My apologies, but I simply couldn't wait another moment to see you."

Grayson's eyes narrowed as he stared at the unwelcome visitor, his body tensing with both annoyance and a primal awareness of her alluring presence. Knox crossed his arms over his broad chest, his expression a mixture of disdain and wariness.

"Your presence here is neither wanted nor appreciated, Eva," Grayson said coldly, his words laced with steel. "Leave now, before I'm forced to make you."

Eva laughed, a sultry, haunting sound that sent shivers down Grayson's spine. She took a step into the room, her movements graceful and predatory, like a panther stalking its prey. "My dear Grayson, you know as well as I do that you lack the power to force me away. And besides," she added, her voice dropping to a husky whisper, "part of you doesn't want me to leave. I can feel it."

As Grayson fought to control his emotions, Knox stepped forward, placing himself between his brother and the seductive vampire. "You're not welcome here, Eva," he repeated firmly, his voice betraying no weakness. "Take your twisted obsession elsewhere."

Eva's eyes seemed to blaze red as she stepped closer, her fingers trailing along the edge of a mahogany table. The dim light from the antique chandelier above danced in her dark, wavy hair, darkening her porcelain skin. "Grayson," she began, her voice low and sultry, "I know you feel that same desire that I do, that unquenchable hunger that has haunted us both for nearly a century now. Raven can never truly satisfy your needs."

Grayson clenched his fists at his sides, struggling to suppress the raw emotions rising within him. He couldn't deny the potency of Eva's presence, the pull of their shared past. But it was Raven who had captured his heart, and he refused to let Eva's manipulations jeopardize that. "You're wrong, Eva," he replied, his tone firm yet measured, betraying none of the turmoil inside him. "Raven is everything I've ever wanted, everything I didn't even know I was searching for. You may have held sway over me once, but those days are long gone."

"Are they, Grayson?" Eva breathed, closing the distance between them until her body brushed against his, the scent of her perfume mingling with the smell of aged bourbon that permeated the air. She tilted her head back to meet his gaze, her lips parting ever so slightly. "I remember our nights together, tangled in each other's arms, lost in a passion so all-consuming it felt as though we were burning alive. Can you honestly say you don't miss that?"

His chest tightened at the memories she evoked, the ghostly sensations of their entwined bodies, their mingled breaths. But Grayson held firm, his resolve was unwavering. "No," he said, his voice low, yet laced with conviction. "What we had was a shadow of what I have with Raven. Our connection is deeper, more meaningful than anything I've ever experienced. And nothing you say or do can change that."

Eva's eyes narrowed, and for a moment, her seductive facade slipped, revealing a glimpse of the fury boiling beneath the surface. "You're making a mistake, Grayson," she hissed, her nails digging into his forearm as she gripped it tightly. "Raven may have bewitched you for now, but in time, you'll see the truth. And when that day comes, I will be waiting."

"Enough!" Grayson snapped, shaking off her grasp and stepping back, placing a barrier of distance between them. "This ends here, Eva. Your twisted games have no place in my life any longer. Leave, and don't come back."

For a moment, it seemed as though Eva might lash out, driven by her wounded pride and thwarted desires. Instead, she regarded him coolly, her expression inscrutable. "Very well," she murmured, her voice once again smooth and composed. "But remember this, Grayson Beaumont—there are some bonds that cannot be broken, some fires that never truly die. You may deny it all you want, but deep down, you know we are destined to be together." With that, she abruptly left, her words lingering in the air like an ominous promise.

The moon hung low in the sky, illuminating small specters that danced across the grounds of the Beaumont estate as Grayson and Knox followed the shadows out onto the front porch. In the haunting silence that followed Eva's departure, Grayson's heart raced with a mix of dread and anger, fueled by the lingering sting of her words. He knew she wouldn't go quietly, not without one final attempt to claim him as her own.

As if summoned by his thoughts, the surrounding air grew cold, and a sinister presence seemed to seep into the very fabric of the night. The scent of blood and roses filled Grayson's nostrils, and he tensed, knowing full well what was about to unfold.

"Did you truly think it would be that easy?" Eva's voice slithered through the darkness, sultry and venomous. Her figure emerged from the shadows, her eyes now glowing a menacing blood-red, and her fangs elongated in a perverse grin. "You know me better than that, darling."

"Stay back, Eva," Grayson warned, his voice steady despite the fear gnawing at the edges of his mind. "I won't let you hurt anyone."

Eva laughed, the sound chilling and devoid of any human warmth. "We'll see about that." And with a flick of her wrist, objects around them levitated—the heavy oak chairs, the ornate silver candlesticks, even the shards of shattered glass—each suspended in mid-air, poised to strike.

"Knox!" Grayson shouted, sensing the danger encroaching upon them. Knox sprang into action, positioning himself between Grayson and the airborne projectiles, his muscles taut with readiness.

"Something's not right," Knox muttered, his brow furrowing as he regarded the scene before them. "She shouldn't have this kind of power. There must be a witch protecting her, feeding her magic."

Grayson's eyes widened at the revelation, but there was no time to process it further as Eva unleashed her attack. The levitating objects hurtled toward Grayson and Knox with deadly precision, their supernatural strength barely enough to deflect the onslaught.

"Pathetic," Eva sneered, her voice dripping with disdain. "You think your devotion to that little witch will protect you? She's nothing compared to the power I wield."

"Leave Raven out of this!" Grayson spat, his fury igniting within him like wildfire. As he dodged and deflected the barrage, he knew he couldn't let Eva harm the woman he loved, nor could he allow her twisted obsession to dictate his fate any longer.

Knox's eyes narrowed as he gauged Eva's next move, his body tensing with anticipation. In a flash, he lunged forward to intercept a flying candlestick aimed at Grayson's head, his quick reflexes and supernatural strength on full display.

"Grayson, watch her!" Knox warned, his voice strained but steady amidst the chaos. His hair whipped around his face, but his eyes remained fixed on the levitating objects, even as they changed directions mid-flight.

"Is this what you've become, Eva?" Grayson gritted out, evading an airborne shard of glass that sliced through the air where he stood moments before. "A pawn of witches and their dark magic?"

Eva laughed coldly; her blood-red eyes gleaming with malice. "Oh, darling, you have no idea."

Unbeknownst to them all, Raven stood rooted to the manor's balcony above, her heart pounding in her chest. She had been drawn to the commotion, curiosity getting the better of herself until she watched the altercation from a hidden vantage point. Her eyes widened in shock as her lips parted to let out a silent gasp, unable to tear her gaze away from the scene unfolding below.

She had known there were other supernatural beings in Bourbon County, but witnessing the raw power and intensity of this confrontation was something entirely different. Thoughts raced through her mind as she tried to comprehend the implications of what she was seeing. How many more like Eva were out there? And what did this mean for her relationship with Grayson?

"Damn it, we need to end this now!" Grayson shouted, frustration edging his voice as he continued to dodge and deflect Eva's relentless assault.

"Agreed," Knox replied gruffly, his focus unwavering as he anticipated the trajectory of another hurtling object, snatching it out of the air.

As Raven watched the brothers standing together, defending each other against the onslaught, her heart swelled with a mixture of fear and admiration. She knew she should step forward, offer her assistance, but fear held her back—the lingering worry about the Witch's Council's disapproval, and her uncertain place in this dangerous world.

"Grayson, look out!" Knox suddenly cried, his eyes widening as he spotted a heavy oak deck chair hurtling toward his brother.

In a split second, Grayson pivoted on his heel to evade the projectile, barely escaping its path as it crashed into the house behind him. His eyes met Knox's for a moment, gratitude flickering within them before they both turned their attention back to Eva.

"Enough!" Grayson roared, his anger and frustration finally reaching a breaking point. "You may have the power of an unnatural witch at your disposal, Eva, but you will never have my heart."

Eva glared at him, rage flaring in her crimson eyes. But despite her fury, she seemed to realize that her efforts were futile. With one last contemptuous snarl, she abruptly ceased her attack, the objects crashing to the ground around them. And just like that, she was gone, retreating from the estate as if she had never been there at all.

As the dust settled, Grayson and Knox exchanged weary glances, their breaths ragged and chests heaving. They had survived the confrontation, but the repercussions of what they had experienced lingered heavy in the air.

Up on the balcony, Raven struggled to process the events she had just witnessed, her mind a whirlwind of emotions. One thing was certain: she could no longer ignore the truth about Grayson and his surrounding world. It was time for answers, and she would not rest until she had them all.

As Grayson and Knox caught their breath, Raven's thoughts raced wildly. She could no longer ignore the dark forces at play here, forces that went far beyond mere immortality. Grayson was more than just an ageless Immortal—he was being hunted. Steeling her nerves with a deep breath, she emerged from her concealed perch on the balcony and descended the stone steps to the moon-washed patio below.

"Grayson," she called, her voice ringing out sharply in the heavy silence.

The brothers whirled in surprise, forgetting about Raven in the heated moments before. As anger showed in their faces before shifting to worry. "Raven,"

Grayson exhaled, his stormy eyes searching hers intently. "I am so sorry you had to witness that…"

"I have a right to know," she cut him off, her gaze boring fiercely into his slate-gray one. "Now I need to understand."

Fat raindrops began to splatter down as Eva's hasty departure left Grayson and Knox alone to reckon with the aftermath. The growing storm echoed the inner turmoil churning within each of them, the night air thick with tension and unspoken fears.

"Raven," Grayson whispered, his heart lurching at the sight of her. Though relief washed over him, he knew they now ventured into dangerous, unmapped territory—a place where secrets could remain hidden no longer.

"Talk to me!" Raven demanded, her eyes flashing with a volatile mix of care and anger. "Tell me everything about your past with Eva and the new threats we now face."

"Okay, okay," Grayson conceded wearily, his piercing gaze reflecting both remorse and resolve. He steeled himself for the coming confrontation, knowing only raw honesty remained. "Eva and I… we were intimate long ago, but it ended wretchedly. She became unhealthily fixated on me, and I've been trying to escape her twisted obsession ever since."

"Obsession?" Raven questioned, brow furrowing as she struggled to fathom Eva's dark compulsions.

"Yes," Grayson affirmed, rubbing his neck anxiously. "I never wanted this cursed life. But meeting you changed everything. You made me feel truly alive again, and I realized I could not let Eva control my fate any longer."

"Is that why she came for us?" Raven pressed, her voice quivering with uncertainty. "Because she sensed your feelings for me?"

"Perhaps," Grayson conceded, jaw tensing involuntarily. "But I will not allow her to hurt you, Raven. You have my word."

"Grayson, I need the whole truth," she insisted, searching his eyes for any deception. "If we're to face this threat together, we can hide nothing more from each other."

"All right," he acquiesced, inhaling deeply to steady himself. "I'll tell you everything, omitting nothing."

As they stood together in the storm, tempests swirling around them like a maelstrom of emotions threatening to engulf them both, Grayson began unburdening his past—the noble, the sinister, the unthinkable. And with each truth revealed, Raven felt their bond deepen further, joining them in a way that transcended mortal bounds.

For what seemed like hours, they sat in the storm, the relentless rain a cold sheet around them as Grayson laid out his immortal life in stark detail. He spoke of his transformation, the pain and bewilderment, and how it had irrevocably changed him and Knox. He confessed his connection with Eva after meeting her in New Orleans in 1950, how manipulation and obsession had twisted an initial attraction into a dangerous bond he had struggled to sever for decades.

Grayson told her tales of how he had turned off all emotions, enjoying the ride of being immortal, drinking until he had his fill—lovely ladies, money, power, and anything else he wanted. Who would stop him from taking any of it?

"I was trying to fill a void I didn't even realize was there...until now," he admitted as he looked at her. Grayson, remembering the past, had turned off his emotions and embraced the darkness within him, indulging in the pleasures of immortality without restraint. Drinking blood to his heart's content, seducing lovely ladies left and right, amassing wealth and power... it's a familiar tale among his kind.

Yet, as he gazed at Raven, her eyes reflecting the soft glow from the manor windows, he felt something stir within him—a forgotten want, a neglected need. In her company, the void that had gnawed at him for decades seemed to recede, replaced by a warmth that he had not felt in a century.

"It was New Orleans in 1950...such a vibrant time. The city has a way of drawing people in and binding them together in ways they never thought possible. My relationship with her, if that is what you want to call it...was twisted and complex, a dangerous bond formed out of manipulation and obsession. It's not surprising now that I have struggled to sever it for decades–such connections can be incredibly difficult to break." Grayson was deep into his story, eyes seeing a different time.

His confession about trying to fill a void...it speaks volumes about the emptiness many immortals feel deep within their souls. "We may have all eternity at our disposal, but that doesn't mean we're immune to feelings of loneliness or discontentment." Grayson smiled wistfully.

"Time may be our playground, but it can also be a prison of sorts. An endless repetition of moments, each one more fleeting than the last," he continued, his voice just above a whisper. His gaze now far away, trapped in the memories of his past.

"The prolonged existence can be a burden, an endless parade of nights where you drown in your own solitude," Grayson confessed further, his piercing gray eyes reflecting a depth of despair Raven couldn't have fathomed.

It was surreal for Raven to witness this vulnerable side of Grayson, a stark contrast to the confident, carefree facade he often projected. Each word he uttered was laden with regret and longing that wrenched at her heart. "It's unnerving to think that immortality can be so…empty."

Grayson nodded solemnly. "That's the irony of it all. On the one hand, you would think the abundance of time would grant us the opportunity to experience everything this world has to offer. But it is precisely this abundance that dilutes the value of those experiences. We lose sight of how precious each moment is when there is always another waiting just around the corner."

"Sometimes, immortality feels like a curse. An endless cycle of dawn and dusk, where old wounds refuse to heal, where time can't wash away the past," Grayson murmured, his piercing eyes clouded with the ghost of those nights.

Eva was enchanting, he admitted, a creature that thrived in the night. But beneath her porcelain skin and mesmerizing amber eyes lurked a darkness that seemed to swallow all light. She was a vampire, driven by a relentless thirst for power and possession.

"Eva has this…power," he confessed, his voice low

but steady. "A power to ensnare the mind and enslave the heart. I was drawn to her, wanting to be consumed...until I realized that was more possession than a true relationship. I wanted liberation."

There was a poignant silence between them; their connection grew deeper as they braved the storm of revelations together. "Does being with me...scare you?" Grayson finally asked, his voice hoarse with vulnerability.

Raven didn't hesitate. "No," she said firmly, her hold on his hand tightening reassuringly. "I'm not scared of you or your past." That was the truth. He did not scare her, after all, witches are not afraid of immortals, but...she feared all he had done, innocent lives he took. She knew she had to ask, though she did not want the answer, but she had to know. He was immortal, so was he still taking lives to feed...

"Grayson..." she began with a hesitant tone, her eyes locked onto his, "do you...take lives?" She couldn't bring herself to say all the words, but he understood, looking away. A heavy silence sat between them again.

He turned back to her slowly, the gravity of her question reflected in his face. His eyes were tormented; there was no hiding that this was a part of him he wished he could separate from. "In the beginning..." he started with a choked voice. "I didn't know how to control it...the need...it's more than hunger; it's like drowning and gasping for air. But that's not who I am now, Raven."

"Then what?" she asked, a wave of relief washing over her as she held onto every word that parted from his lips.

"I learned how to survive without taking an innocent life," he confessed. His gaze returned to hers—sincere and pleading for her to understand. "It wasn't easy, but Knox and I... we managed, with time." He took a deep breath, and went on, "we know other witches, one in New Orleans set me up with a magical recipe that helps. Less blood needed in our 'diets'." He tried to laugh, though he soon realized it was not all that funny.

The horror had lifted from her eyes, replaced by an understanding that comforted him more than he could have imagined. "So, if you could, would you go back to being...normal?"

His gaze softened and a sad smile pulled at the corners of his mouth. "If I could turn back time, I would do it all differently. But this is who I am now, Raven," he said with a sigh. "And I can't change what was done."

"I see," she whispered, and gave his hand a gentle squeeze. Her silence lasted only a moment before her curiosity bubbled over once again. "And Eva?"

Her question hung in the air like a ghost, its icy touch making Grayson shudder. "Eva..." he began reluctantly, his voice laced with bitterness. "She was...is...a vampire. She loved the power it gave her...loved playing with her victims before draining them." His expression turned grim as he continued. "I thought we had more in common when we first met. But I soon realized our definitions of 'fun' were vastly different."

"But all that...all those dark years...they mean nothing in the light of what I feel for you, Raven," Grayson confessed, his piercing eyes mirroring the storm's intensity with a fervor of their own. "You've awakened something in me. A desire not just for survival, but to truly live. To cherish every sunrise, every moonlit night…with you."

The intensity of his gaze unsettled her, yet she did not look away. There was something deeply touching about his words, something that made her heart flutter dangerously in her chest. "Grayson…" she breathed, her mind reeling from the surge of emotions coursing through her veins.

"I know it's a lot to take in," he admitted, reaching out to tuck a stray lock of hair behind her ear. His touch was gentle, almost reverent, sending shivers down her spine. "But I need you to understand why I have done what I did—my past, is not pretty, hasn't been for a long time—I fully embraced the dark side of this life."

Raven had listened, her heart pounding with a mix of fear, fascination, and a strange sense of relief. For the first time, she felt like she was seeing the real Grayson—not just the chiseled good looks and charm, but the angst that lay beneath his confident facade.

They sat there, side by side, in a charged silence. The rain had tapered off to drizzle, leaving the world hushed and dew-kissed in the early pre-dawn hour. Raven looked at him—really looked—and saw not only an immortal with a tormented past, but also a man who longed for love and freedom just as much as she did.

Finally, Raven smiled and said, "Let's go inside."

As they stepped inside, the crisp evening air gave way to the warm comfort of the manor. Grayson pulled her close to him. He looked down into her eyes, reflecting the soft glow of the lights above. He leaned down slowly, pressing his lips against hers in a tender kiss.

Their pasts may have been filled with darkness—uninvited immortality on one side and witchcraft on the other—but standing there beneath the cathedral ceiling, they knew they'd found light in each other amidst rifts of supernatural worlds.

"I'm sorry," Grayson whispered, finally standing back from her. "I should have told you everything sooner."

Raven reached out to take his hand, her touch gentle yet firm. "It's okay. I can't imagine it was easy for you...living through all that." She squeezed his hand reassuringly. "What if Eva returns?"

"Then we'll deal with it," he vowed, his gaze filled with unwavering determination. "No matter what, Raven, I will always choose you, and this life. No more lost dark days."

As the storm slowly died out, the two lovers stood united against the coming darkness, their bodies close together, their hearts aflame. The memory of Eva and her vampiric rage seemed to fade away in the sanctuary of the manor. It was replaced by the promise of shared secrets, hushed talks under the soft glow of the fire, and stolen kisses that tasted like sweet bourbon.

The front door creaked open, revealing Knox's tall, brooding figure in the dim light. Without a word, he slipped out into the night, leaving Grayson and Raven to confront their pasts and forge a new path together.

"Where is he going?" Raven asked, watching Knox's retreating form with concern.

"Knox needs time to clear his mind," Grayson explained, a hint of sadness in his eyes. "He cares deeply for both of us, but sometimes he finds it difficult to navigate the complexities of our world and the relationships in it."

As the door closed behind Knox, Grayson pulled Raven closer, wrapping her in the safety of his embrace.

"Grayson," she murmured, her breath warm against his chest. "Promise me you'll never let Eva come between us."

"Raven, I swear on my immortal soul that nothing, not Eva, or any threat that may come our way, will ever come between us," he vowed, sealing his promise with a searing kiss that ignited the fire within them both.

And as they lost themselves in each other's arms, the darkness of the world outside seemed to fade away, replaced by the unbreakable bond that bound their hearts together for eternity. Fate was taking over, outside forces pushing them together.

The flickering flames of the fireplace cast a warm glow on Grayson's face, illuminating the vulnerability that lay beneath his usual confident demeanor. As Raven nestled into the crook of his arm, she couldn't help but be struck by the depth of emotion reflected in his perfect ocean eyes, the same eyes that had captivated her from the moment they met.

Grayson leaned down to capture her lips in a fiery, passionate kiss that left them both breathless. His hands roamed her body, reigniting the smoldering desire that burned between them. The feel of his fingers tracing the curve of her hips sent shivers down her spine, igniting a primal need within her.

"Make love to me, Grayson," she whispered, her voice thick with desire. "Show me that our love can conquer the darkness."

With a growl of longing, he swept her up into his arms and carried her upstairs to his bed, the intensity of his gaze never leaving her. In the dimly lit sanctuary, he gently sat her on the bed. Her raven hair spilled out around her like a midnight halo, and her emerald eyes shimmered with a passion mirroring his own. He explored her body, his touch feather-light, as if memorizing every curve and line.

As Grayson's lips trailed a searing path down her neck, the heat of his touch sent shivers of anticipation through her. He growled low in his throat at the evidence of her arousal.

Raven arched her back, giving him better access, as he nibbled and sucked at her hardened nipples. His touch was like a fiery caress, igniting a passionate anticipation within her.

Grayson felt Raven's desire, and it only fueled his own. He slipped his hand beneath her dress, finding the edge of her panties. He hooked his fingers under the elastic and slowly pulled them down her legs, his eyes never leaving hers. He groaned, feeling the slick wetness between her thighs. He cupped her sex, his fingers slipping easily inside of her.

Raven gasped as Grayson's fingers stroked her in just the right way. 'She reached down and began to unbutton Grayson's pants, desperate to feel him inside of her.

Grayson kicked off his pants, and he wasted no time positioning himself between Raven's legs. Heat radiated off her skin, and the primal urge to be inside her intensified. He pushed inside of her with one swift motion, causing them both to cry out in pleasure.

Raven's nails scraped against Grayson's back as he

thrust inside her. He started off slowly, savoring the feel of her tightness around him. But soon, they were both lost in rhythm, their bodies moving in perfect harmony.

Grayson felt Raven's muscles clenching around him, signaling her impending orgasm. He thrust harder and deeper, wanting to feel her come apart around him. And when she finally did, it was like nothing he had ever felt before. He followed soon after, his own release shaking him to his core.

As they lay there, spent and panting, Grayson looked down at Raven, feeling a warmth spread through his chest. He knew at that moment that he had fallen in love with her, and he would do anything to make her happy. Anything!

Slowly disentangling himself from her, he pressed a tender kiss to her forehead before rising from the bed. He pulled on his clothes with unhurried ease, all the while keeping his eyes on her. Despite having shared in the most intimate of acts, he felt a new shyness blossom between them—a delightful tenderness that made his ribs ache sweetly.

She lazily draped the sheet over her bare body, her eyes alight with an inner glow that left Grayson breathless. No one had ever looked at him like that, as though he were the only man in the world.

"Bourbon?" he asked, gesturing to a dusty bottle on the dresser. It was an old tradition in the Beaumont family, one that they often indulged in after moments of heightened emotion.

Raven smiled, the corners of her lips lifting in amusement as she nodded. "Sounds perfect."

He poured them two glasses of aged bourbon, his

favorite reserve saved for special occasions. The golden liquid glowed under the soft lighting of the room, casting prismatic rainbows against their naked skin as they clinked their glasses together.

"To us," Grayson toasted softly, watching as Raven's eyes crinkled with happiness.

"To us," Raven echoed and drank deeply.

As the rich taste of bourbon hit their tongues, followed by the comforting burn in their throats, they found themselves sinking into a comfortable silence once more. It was a new kind of intimacy between them—quiet and serene yet undeniably charged with desire and longing.

Later, they fell asleep to the sound of crickets outside the window, their bodies curled against each other as though trying to meld into one. Grayson's last thought before surrendering himself to sleep was that he would do anything to protect this woman next to him. Anything...even at the risk of his own eternal life.

And as Raven watched him drift off to sleep, she vowed that when the time came, she would stand by Grayson's side—no matter the cost.

****

Across town, Eva was seething. The scent of Raven on Grayson's clothes still clung to her senses, a cruel affirmation of their connection. Her head throbbed painfully with each heartbeat, but she took in the pain as though it were a penance, a tribute to her unrequited love. She paced around the luxurious penthouse she had compelled her way into, her sharp heels clicking against the marble floor in a maddening rhythm.

Her eyes reflected the flickering city lights outside of her window, their glow only enhancing the unearthly beauty that she possessed. Her twisted obsession with Grayson had led her down a path where she found herself trapped between love and madness. And she had to admit, it was intoxicating.

With forced calmness, Eva poured herself a drink. The dark liquid swirled ominously in the crystal glass, reflecting her tumultuous emotions. She raised the glass in an ironic toast to Grayson and his new lover. "To you both," she smirked bitterly before downing it in one go.

The high-end bourbon burned its way down her throat but did nothing to quell the fire raging inside her. She was not about to let Grayson slip from her grasp so easily. If he wouldn't choose her willingly, then she'd make him regret his decision.

After all, if there's one thing Eva was good at besides seduction, it was manipulation.

Chapter 6

Morning sunlight filtered through the sheer curtains, casting a warm golden glow over the room as Raven stirred awake. The enticing aroma of fresh coffee and a hint of bacon wafted through the air, drawing her from the depths of slumber. She blinked sleepily, her eyes taking in Grayson's bedroom as she stretched luxuriously, the oversized sweater she wore grazing the tops of her thighs.

"Good morning," Grayson murmured, his voice rough with sleep. He appeared relaxed and at ease, his athletic frame clad in a soft, gray henley and dark jeans. His jet-black hair fell in effortless waves, perfectly framing his chiseled jawline and high cheekbones. His piercing blue-gray eyes, often described as windows to the soul, were warm and affectionate as he gazed at her.

"Morning," Raven replied, a playful edge and a hint of sarcasm in her tone. They exchanged sleepy smiles and tender kisses, savoring the intimacy of the moment.

Grayson rose from the chair. "I took the liberty of bringing us breakfast in bed." He gestured to the tray laden with two steaming mugs of coffee, plates piled with eggs and bacon, and a small vase of wildflowers. "Wixx made it for us."

"Thank you," Raven whispered.

As they ate, Raven's thoughts were on her family

history, and felt a deep-rooted urge to share her world with Grayson. Uncharacteristically open and vulnerable, she sought to strengthen their bond and learn from her ancestors.

Hesitantly, she said, "Grayson, I want you to meet my dad. I think it's important for you to see where I come from, the roots from which I grew…And maybe he can give us some advice about the witch's council if they do reach out to me."

His eyes lit up with genuine interest. "I would be honored to meet your father, Raven," Grayson replied earnestly. "I want to learn more about your world, your family history, and your magical heritage."

Raven forced a smile, her heart torn between falling for this man and the fear of revealing her full past. As they finished their breakfast, she could not help but dread what lay ahead: a journey into the depths of her secrets, intertwined with the fire of their forbidden love. But Raven could not shake the urge to keep her true feelings hidden, knowing the consequences if anyone were to discover their passion.

The morning sun cast a warm, golden glow through the bedroom window as Grayson buttoned up his shirt, his gaze lingering on Raven for a moment. "I can't wait to meet your father, Raven." His voice was filled with genuine enthusiasm. "And why don't you invite Marley and Madison too? I would love to get to know them better as well."

Raven's eyes sparkled at the suggestion, and she reached for her phone to send a quick message to her friends. The thought of introducing Grayson to her loved ones filled her with an odd mixture of excitement and nervousness, yet she knew it was a necessary step in their relationship.

Within an hour, Marley and Madison arrived at the Beaumont estate, greeting Raven and Grayson with warm hugs and excited chatter. "Well, sugar, I've got to say, this is one adventure I didn't see comin'," Marley drawled playfully, her Southern charm shining through.

"Speak for yourself, Mar," Madison chimed in with a teasing grin. "I knew these two were destined for something special from the moment I met Grayson. Now, let us hit the road before we lose daylight."

As they climbed into Grayson's car, the four friends exchanged pleasantries and engaged in light-hearted banter, creating a warm and welcoming atmosphere that eased any lingering tension. Raven glanced over at Grayson, who listened to Marley and Madison's playful teasing. She could sense his eagerness, not only to meet her father but also to prove himself to those who mattered most to her.

As they drove through the picturesque Kentucky countryside, Raven found herself lost in thought, reflecting on the whirlwind journey that had brought her to this moment. Her heart swelled with affection for Grayson, the intriguing immortal who had stolen her heart and challenged everything she thought she knew about love and destiny.

"Hey, you, okay?" Grayson asked softly, his fingertips brushing against Raven's as he reached for the gear shift. She glanced over at him, her eyes meeting his in a silent exchange of reassurance and affection.

"I'm more than okay," Raven whispered, squeezing his hand gently. "I'm just grateful to have you, and my friends in my life. It means so much to me."

With a warm smile, Grayson entwined his fingers with hers, their connection deepening with every mile that brought them closer to Raven's family farm—and the mysteries that awaited them there.

The sun's warm golden glow cut across the lush green fields surrounding the charming farmhouse. As the group arrived, a sense of tranquility settled over them, the magical energy of the land weaving its way into their hearts and souls.

Standing on the porch, Raven's father cut an imposing figure, his tall, lean frame a testament to years of hard work and perseverance. The wisdom etched into the lines of his weathered face was unmistakable, as were the curiosity and hint of skepticism that danced in his eyes as he looked at Grayson. But when his gaze fell upon Raven, his features softened, and love radiated from every pore of his being.

"Hey, Dad," Raven called out, her voice filled with warmth and affection. "I want you to meet Grayson."

As they approached, Grayson could not help but feel a mixture of awe and apprehensiveness. He knew how much this moment meant to Raven and wanted nothing more than to make a good impression on the man who had played such a pivotal role in shaping her into the woman she was today.

"Grayson Beaumont, sir," he said, extending his hand for a firm handshake. "It's truly an honor to meet you."

"Morgan Ballard, it is good to meet you. Raven has told me quite a bit about you," her father replied, his grip strong and unyielding as he assessed Grayson with a mix of protectiveness and curiosity. "You have some big shoes to fill, young man."

"Believe me, sir, I know." Grayson chuckled nervously, his mind racing as he searched for the right words to convey his sincerity. "But I promise you, my intentions toward Raven are nothing but genuine."

Raven's father held his gaze for a moment longer before nodding.' "Well then, welcome to our family farm." He gestured for them to come inside. "Let's get to know each other better."

As they stepped into the cozy farmhouse, Grayson could not help but marvel at the sense of history and heritage that permeated every corner. He could feel the weight of generations of love and tradition in the very walls, and it only served to deepen his appreciation for Raven and the roots from which she grew.

"Your home is beautiful," Grayson remarked, his eyes glancing around the room as he soaked in the details—the well-worn wooden floors, the heirloom photographs adorning the walls, and the herbs hanging from the rafters, their earthy scent filling the air.

"Thank you," Morgan replied, a hint of pride in his voice. "It's been in our family for generations."

As they settled into the living room, a strange mix of excitement and nervousness bubbled up within Grayson. He knew that this evening would serve as the foundation for his relationship with Raven's father, and even the key to unlocking the mysteries of the Witch's Council.

"Sir, I hope you don't mind me saying so, but I'm truly captivated by your family's history and connection to this land," Grayson admitted, his curiosity piqued. "I'd love to learn more about your magical heritage, if you'd be willing to share."

Morgan studied him for a moment, then nodded slowly, a small smile playing on his lips. "Very well, Grayson. We will get to all that, soon enough…"

Marley and Madison's infectious laughter filled the air as they stepped into the living room from the porch, their eyes alight with excitement.

"Darlin', it has been too long!" Marley wrapped Raven's father in a tight hug. "You ain't aged a day, sugar."

"He will forever be a spring chicken," Madison chimed in with a playful grin, nudging him gently with her elbow. The rapport between them was undeniable years of shared memories and inside jokes creating an atmosphere of warmth and familiarity.

"Girls, stop picking on him." Raven laughed, her voice tinged with pride. "Grayson, please excuse Marley and Madison. They love to give Dad a hard time."

"I think it is nice how you all are so close," Grayson said, offering a genuine smile.

"See, it is nice," Marley replied, her gaze set on him as though gauging his honesty. "We've been friends too long; this is our home too." She stuck her tongue out at Raven.

Grayson laughed. "Good friends are important," he said, his confident demeanor shining through.

"Yes," Madison responded coyly, her light blue eyes glinting with mischief. "Who else can you cause trouble with and share everything with?"

Her response brought more laughter to the group while they settled into the cozy living room. The conversation flowed effortlessly, punctuated by bursts of laughter and the faint clink of ice cubes in glasses of sweet tea. Morgan regaled them with tales of their magical heritage, describing the ancient ley lines beneath their land and the powerful energies they held.

"Raven's ancestors were some of the first witches to settle here," her father explained, his voice laced with reverence. "They recognized the potential in these lands and dedicated their lives to nurturing the magic within."

Grayson listened intently, his piercing gaze never leaving Raven's father's face. "So, the magic here is unique to your bloodline?"

"It is." He nodded. "Our connection to the land runs deep, and with it comes a responsibility to preserve our traditions."

"Can anyone learn to tap into these energies?" Grayson asked, his curiosity on full display.

"Only those with an affinity for the ley lines," Raven's father replied. "However, some immortals with strong connections to the land may be able to access this magic as well, though vampires cannot."

The day moved slowly, as most do in the summer months in Kentucky. And as the sun dipped below the horizon, casting dancing lights across the room, Grayson found himself increasingly captivated by this new world unfolding before him. He felt a sense of belonging that had been absent for far too long, igniting within him a quiet determination to not only protect Raven but also to honor her family's legacy as she stated she would his.

In the soft twilight, with the scent of magnolia blossoms drifting through the open windows, Grayson knew one thing for certain—his feelings for Raven were growing stronger by the moment, and he would stop at nothing to safeguard their intertwined destinies.

The light of the sun shone through the thick canopy of old trees, creating a beautiful dance of patterns on the ground with alternating patches of light and shadow. Grayson and Raven walked hand in hand along a narrow path, their fingers intertwined as if to anchor themselves to one another amidst the enchanting landscape.

"Tell me about this place," Grayson murmured, his voice barely audible above the whisper of leaves rustling overhead. His eyes, filled with longing and affection, never left Raven's face.

Raven smiled, her eyes sparkling with a mix of pride and nostalgia. "The farm has been in my family for generations, like Dad said," she explained. "It's protected by a magical seal, which keeps our world hidden from those who might wish to exploit its power. Here we can be truly free."

As they continued their exploration, pausing occasionally to admire the vibrant wildflowers or marvel at the intricate web of roots that weaved the very earth together, Grayson felt an overwhelming sense of wonder. The beauty of nature—untamed and raw—echoed in his heart, resonating with the magic that flowed through Raven's veins.

Later, as twilight descended like a velvet blanket over the farm, the group gathered around a rustic wooden table laden with a feast of farm-fresh delights. Laughter and conversation filled the air, creating a warm, welcoming atmosphere that seemed to wrap itself around the hearts of everyone present.

Yet, it was during this shared meal that Grayson found himself compelled to open about his own past.

The truth about his immortality, the sacrifices made by his family to protect him and Knox, all weighed on his soul, begging to be released into the understanding embrace of those who now felt like family.

"I haven't always been...like this," he began hesitantly, his gaze shifting between Raven, her father, Marley, and Madison. "My brother Knox and I were ambushed by a mysterious immortal while transporting bourbon for our grandmother. We were transformed into immortals ourselves, with enhanced abilities. It was a painful, bewildering experience."

As Grayson spoke, the others listened intently, their eyes filled with understanding and empathy. Raven reached over to gently squeeze his hand, offering silent support as he continued to divulge the secrets of his heart.

"Since then, we've struggled to hide our true nature from the human world," he confessed, a hint of sadness in his voice. "It's complicated our personal and business lives...but meeting Raven has changed everything for me."

In the firelight that flickered across their faces, Grayson could see the unspoken acceptance and compassion that lay within each pair of eyes focused on him. And as they shared stories long into the night, the weight of his past lightened, replaced by the warmth of newfound connections, all tinged with the heady magic of love.

Raven's father leaned back in his chair, fixing his gaze on his daughter. The creases around his eyes deepened as he reached out to place a reassuring hand on her shoulder.

"Raven, I know you're worried about the Witch's

Council," he said softly, his voice carrying the wisdom of years spent navigating the complexities of their magical world. "If they reach out, just remember that old witches can be fickle." He winked at Grayson, who chuckled despite the tension in the air. "They may understand that some things are out of our control, like finding a partner in the most unusual way or a nosy vampire stirring up trouble whom you could not control. You never know what they will do. Maybe you can make them see that times have changed, and old rules sometimes need to change too."

"Thanks, Dad." Raven offered a small smile, taking comfort in his guidance. She knew her father's experience would be invaluable when it came to dealing with the council and their unpredictable ways.

The evening ended, and the group moved to gather around closer to the crackling bonfire. Shadows danced across their faces as they settled into their seats, the flickering flames casting an enchanting glow on the scene. In the distance, the silhouettes of trees and rolling land stood against a sky dotted with stars, creating a serene backdrop for the intimate gathering.

The scent of burning wood mingled with the soft whispers of the wind, carrying the promise of autumn and the deepening connection between Raven and Grayson. He could not help but steal glances at her, captivated by the way the firelight played on her features and those eyes that held a world of mystery and magic.

"Raven, thank you for this," Grayson said, reaching for her hand, and interlocking their fingers. His heart raced as she turned to face him, their bodies gravitating toward each other like two celestial bodies drawn together by an unbreakable force.

"Grayson, always," she whispered back, her breath warm on his skin as she leaned in, her eyes locked with his. As their lips met in a sweet kiss, the world around them seemed to fade away, leaving only the heat of the fire and the intensity of their connection.

Raven's heart pounded in her chest, her senses heightened by the magic that surrounded them and the love that was beginning to take root in the fertile soil of their hearts. Grayson's hands traced delicate patterns on her back, his touch sending shivers of desire down her spine.

As they pulled apart, their gazes held each other, unwilling to let go of the moment. They knew that the challenges ahead would assess their connection, but for now, they basked in the fire's warmth and the unspoken promise that their souls were entwining beneath the starlit sky.

After more shared stories, the group decided to call it a night. Grayson offered his car to Madison and Marley when Raven suggested he see her place. Many heartfelt hugs and goodbyes later, the night embraced the farm in a velvety darkness, punctuated by the gentle chorus of crickets and the distant hoots of owls. Guided by the silvery glow of the full moon, Grayson and Raven walked hand in hand toward her cottage, nestled at the edge of the farm. The air was thick with the scent of honeysuckle and lingering traces of bonfire smoke, adding an earthy sensuality to the atmosphere.

"Raven," Grayson whispered as he pushed open the cottage door, his voice rough with desire. "I've never felt this way before."

"Neither have I," she admitted, her cheeks flushed

with a mix of anticipation and vulnerability. They stepped inside the dimly lit cottage, their fingers still entwined.

As the door closed behind them, Grayson gently backed Raven against the wall, his body pressing into hers with insistent hunger. A fiery kiss ignited between them, their tongues tangling together, seeking to possess the essence of the other. Grayson's hands roamed her body, tracing the curves that had haunted his dreams since their first encounter.

"Grayson," Raven moaned, her nails digging into his shoulders as he dipped his head to nibble on her neck. Heat rose within her.

"Tell me you want this," he whispered against her skin, his breath hot and ragged. The plea in his voice resonated deep within her, echoing the same longing that had been growing inside her all day.

"More than anything," she breathed, her voice etched with a fervent sincerity, fierce and unwavering.

With a groan of satisfaction, Grayson lifted her into his arms, his fingers digging into the soft flesh of her hips. He could not believe the desire coursing through his veins, his body demanding release from the tension that had been growing all day. Her eyes locked onto his, and he could see the same longing reflected in their depths.

"I want you so bad," he growled, his lips crushing against hers in a hungry kiss. His tongue teased her bottom lip, coaxing her mouth open, and he groaned as she eagerly responded.

Their tongues danced together, a slow and sensual rhythm that mirrored the building heat between their bodies. Grayson's hand slid up her back, tracing the curve of her spine before tangling in her hair. He tugged gently, tilting her head back and exposing her neck to his hungry kisses. Fighting the urge to bite.

He nipped and suckled at the delicate skin, his teeth grazing over her pulse point. She gasped, her body quivering in his arms. "Grayson," she breathed, her voice husky with desire.

He carried her to the bed, their lips never breaking contact. The moonlight cast a soft, ethereal glow across the room, illuminating their entwined bodies. Grayson laid her down gently, his body covering hers as he deepened their kiss.

His hands roamed over her curves, exploring every inch of her body as if it were the first time. She arched into his touch, her own hands gripping his shoulders. The feel of her soft skin beneath his fingertips was intoxicating, and Grayson could not resist the urge to taste more of her.

He trailed kisses down her neck, his tongue darting out to taste the salty sweetness of her skin. Her breasts were heavy and full, and he cupped them, his thumbs teasing her nipples into hard peaks. She moaned, her back arching off the bed as pleasure coursed through her body.

Grayson's lips continued their descent, kissing and licking a path down her stomach until he reached the waistband of her jeans. He hooked his fingers into the denim and tugged, sliding them down her legs and tossing them aside. His gaze traveled over her body, drinking in the sight of her in nothing but her lacy underwear.

"You're so beautiful," he murmured, his voice rough with desire.

She bit her lip causing a single drip of blood to escape, Grayson felt his primal need in that drop, but when her eyes locked onto his as she reached for the button of his jeans, his whole body went into overdrive—wanting her. He helped her with his pants, sliding them down his legs until he was naked before her. He was ready, throbbing with need, and she wrapped her hand around him, stroking him slowly.

Grayson hissed, his hips bucking involuntarily at her touch. He could feel the tension coiling in his lower body, the pressure building with every stroke. He wanted nothing more than to bury himself inside her, to feel her warmth surrounding him.

But he wanted to make this last. He wanted to savor every moment, every sensation. He wanted to make her feel good, to make her scream his name. To want only ever to be with him, a longing that ached in his chest like a persistent throb.

He pushed her gently onto her back, his mouth finding hers once again as he slid her underwear down her legs. He spread her thighs apart, his fingers tracing a path up her inner thigh until he reached her slick heat.

She was already wet for him, and he groaned at the feeling of her. He teased her with his thumb, his fingers sliding inside her. She was tight, and he could feel her muscles clenching around him. He pumped his fingers in and out, his thumb rubbing circles over just the right spot as he kissed her deeply.

She moaned, her hips bucking as wave after wave of pleasure washed over her. He felt her getting closer and closer to the edge, her body coiled tight like a spring.

When Grayson finally slid inside her, it was like

nothing he had ever felt before. He filled her completely; he was hitting all the right spots. She gasped, her nails digging into his back as he thrust.

Their bodies moved together in a slow and deliberate rhythm, each stroke sending sparks of pleasure shooting through his body. Tension built, her muscles tightening around him as she approached the edge.

Grayson's lips were everywhere, kissing at her neck, shoulders, and breasts.

When she finally came, it was like an explosion of pleasure. She cried out his name, her body shuddering as wave after wave of ecstasy washed over her. Grayson followed shortly after, his own release leaving him breathless and spent.

They lay there for a moment, their bodies entwined, their breathing heavy. Grayson kissed her gently, his lips lingering on hers as they basked in the afterglow of their lovemaking.

It was a slow and deliberate build, a deep and physical connection that left them both breathless and satisfied. It was hot and sweet, a perfect blend of passion and love. Something Grayson had never truly experienced before. His need for her was greater than his need for blood.

Grayson's fingers traced intricate patterns on her skin, igniting a new trail of fire in their wake. Raven responded to his every move, her own hands exploring the planes of his body with a mix of tenderness and urgency.

"Raven," Grayson gasped as their bodies moved ever so closer together, their souls dancing in a rhythm older than time itself. "You're my everything."

Tears pricked at the corners of Raven's eyes as she clung to him, overwhelmed by the intensity of their connection. "And you are mine, Grayson."

As the night wore on, they lost themselves in each other, whispers of passion and desire echoing through the moonlit cottage. Time seemed to stand still, honoring the sacred union between two souls destined to be intertwined.

With the dawn still hours away, Grayson and Raven lay entwined in each other's arms, their bodies bathed in the soft glow of moonlight filtering through the windows. In the quiet sanctuary of their own world, they exchanged tender words and hopeful dreams, their hearts beginning to intertwine in a love that defied the boundaries of time, one that was fated to withstand whatever trials lay ahead.

"Whatever happens," Grayson murmured into Raven's hair, his voice thick with emotion, "I want you to know that I'll fight for us, for this."

"Me too," she whispered back, her heart swelling with a fierce determination to protect what they had found together. "Together is where I always want to be."

As the first light of dawn crept through the curtains, Raven's heart weighed heavy with the knowledge that they must face the Witch's Council. She knew deep down, waiting for them would drive her mad. Stirring gently in Grayson's embrace, she met his gaze, her emerald eyes shimmering with unspoken resolve.

"Grayson," she whispered, her voice barely audible, "I think it's time we approach the council. We need to deal with this head on."

He studied her face for a moment, his eyes filled with a mixture of love and concern, before nodding in agreement. "Whatever you want to do. I will go with you, Raven. No matter what happens, at least we are together."

They dressed in silence, the tension between them thick as they prepared to confront the unknown. As they stood at the threshold of the cottage, Raven turned to Grayson, her fingers brushing against his cheek in a tender caress. Their lips met in a lingering kiss, a silent vow sealing their intertwined destinies.

"Let's go," she said softly, taking his hand and leading him out into the crisp morning air.

The sun had risen higher by the time they reached the front of the farm, casting long shadows across the lush green fields. To their surprise, the counsel's three elders were already there, standing alongside Raven's father on the porch of the farmhouse. Their stern faces bespoke both judgment and uncertainty, hinting at the gravity of the situation.

"Raven, and Grayson, I presume," the eldest witch greeted, her voice cold as ice. "We have heard your intentions, and we are here to discuss the terms and conditions under which our council may allow your union."

A heated debate ensued between the other two elders and Raven, each side arguing their case with fierce conviction. Raven's father stood by her side, lending his wisdom and support as they navigated the complexities of the witches' traditions and the council's fears.

After a few moments, the eldest stated, "I think we will allow this, for now. Excuse us as we discuss the terms of which it will be upheld." With a wave of her hand, the three seemed to disappear. Grayson stood, motionless, unsure of what to expect.

Moments later, the three elders appeared before them, standing in unison only looking at Raven. What seemed like forever, before the eldest witch stepped forward and spoke to them.

"Ultimately," the eldest witch said, her eyes narrowing as she regarded Raven and Grayson, "it is clear that your connection is powerful, but it must be evaluated. We have set forth a series of guidelines to ensure the strength and purity of your bond."

"Remember," another elder added, her voice gentler, "the consequences of your actions reach beyond yourselves. Your union could change the course of our world."

As they faced the elders, hand in hand, Raven and Grayson's hearts beat together, a testament to their blossoming love. They would face these trials together for the sake of their love and the future it held. Their intertwined destinies hung in the balance, a challenge that would test not only their passion but also their courage and the very essence of who they were. The path ahead was uncertain, but one thing was clear: they would walk it side by side, supported by the connection that bound them together, no matter what happens.

The moving of clouds overhead caused the sun to sway in and out of sight, leaving long shadows that hinted at the mysteries hidden beneath the surface of all it touched. Raven and Grayson stood side by side, silhouetted against the dying morning, their gazes locked on the departing figures of the Witch's Council elders.

"Raven," Grayson murmured, his voice low and laced with concern. "These conditions…do you think we will be able to honor them all?"

Raven hesitated. "I don't know," she admitted, her hand tightening around his. "But I'm not afraid to face them or anything else, as long as you are standing by me."

Their fingers intertwined, forming an unbreakable bond that echoed the love that had blossomed between them.

"Grayson," she whispered, her voice mixing with the rustling leaves, "I can feel it—something dark is stirring, and I fear it is getting closer to us."

He pulled her to him, wrapping his protective arms around her. "I can manage dark. I have been there many times, Raven. What I could never handle is you ever leaving me."

In the distance, a lone owl hooted mournfully, its haunting call echoing through the night like a ghostly warning. The world held its breath, waiting for the moment when darkness would descend and force them to confront the unknown darkness that awaited them.

"Me, leave you? Never," Raven whispered, her eyes searching Grayson's, seeking reassurance amidst the gathering shadows. "Promise me that no matter what happens, you'll never let me go."

"Never," he vowed, sealing his promise with an enthusiastic kiss that sent shivers down her spine and ignited a flame within her soul. "I will never let you go, Raven. We will always be together. You are my light in this world, and I intend to follow it forever!"

Back in the farmhouse, Morgan Ballard watched them from a window, his worn eyes reflecting a curious blend of concern and hope. His calloused hands gripped an old wooden cane adorned with intricate symbols—a testament to their magical heritage. Seeing his daughter with Grayson stirred a strong emotion in his heart—an irrevocable acceptance of a love that defied conventions.

Morgan turned away from the window, the soft creak of the wooden floor marking his slow procession toward the hearth. The fire had burned down to its embers. Picking up an old photograph, he traced his finger over the faces smiling back at him. Even then, he knew Raven was incredibly special—her green eyes held a spark that set her apart. He knew her powers were going to be strong. Now she was in love with an immortal, and it was about to change everything. Oh, how he wished her mother was alive to be here, to help guide this.

His thoughts were interrupted as Raven entered the house, her dark hair disheveled from the wind outside and her expression thoughtful. She had a stubborn streak and independent spirit. Yet around her family, her softer side emerged. Her eyes, dancing in the dim light of the fading fire, met Morgan's with a look of comprehension.

"You saw us," she said, her voice a whisper. "Together outside. You are worried?"

Morgan sighed heavily, his gaze returning to the photograph in his hand. "Yes. You all have chosen a path that will test you in ways we cannot even begin to imagine. The days ahead are going to be filled with uncertainty."

"But we are falling in love with each other, Father," Raven interjected, moving closer to drape an arm around his broad shoulders. "Doesn't that count for anything?"

Morgan smiled wistfully, the corners of his mouth revealing lines etched by time and trials. "My dear child," he began softly, "love is a powerful force indeed. But it can't shield you both from everything."

Raven turned away, gazing out at the silhouetted figure of Grayson in the garden, looking at the herbs under the soft glow of flickering lanterns.

"Then we must do what we can to protect all of us." Raven spoke to her father with confidence she did not truly believe she had.

She turned back to face her father, her expressive green eyes shining with determination. "We will face it all. I must, I am falling in love with him. And that has to count for something."

Morgan looked at his daughter, a pang of admiration in his heart. "Raven, my dear," he said, "I never doubted your resolve or your feelings for him. Just be sure that Grayson is equally prepared for the darkness that is about to come. I will speak to our fellow witches to throw a protection spell, so the land will give us strength until the light returns."

Raven understood. He felt the same energy rolling in. It was a weird undercurrent in the ground beneath their feet that was traveling through them, warning them.

Walking back into the garden, Raven found Grayson. He was standing still, his tall form silhouetted against the pale moonlight, staring into the far distance. For a moment, she simply watched him, appreciating the sight of this man in her world. Something stirred deep within her at this site; a longing so profound it left her breathless.

"Grayson?" she called softly, not wanting to startle him from his thoughts.

He turned to face her and the intensity in his gaze took her aback. "Raven..." his voice was low, husky. He crossed the distance between them in just a few strides and enveloped her in his arms, pulling her close.

"I heard your father's words," he confessed. His fingers traced a path down her spine, sending shivers of anticipation through her body. She melted into him as he lowered his lips to hers in a slow, languorous kiss.

"You don't have to worry about me," he said, finally breaking the silence that had settled around them. His words hung between them, heavy with promise and resignation. "I am more than prepared for whatever comes."

Raven looked up at him, her heart pounding. His declaration warmed her like no spell ever could. The raw honesty in his voice made her believe him.

As she leaned against him, their hearts beating like one under the glimmering moonlit sky, Raven felt the surge of magic beneath them, humming with life and energy. It was a reminder of what they stood to lose...and what they could gain if they dared challenge what awaited them.

In that single embrace under the stars, Raven realized what must be done. They needed to trust not just each other, but also their own powers. The magic that ran through their veins and the love that was budding between them might just be their strongest weapon in the battles to come.

As they returned to Raven's cottage, hand in hand, a new resolve glimmered in their eyes. They would face the darkness together. And as they lost themselves in another passionate night, it was with a sense of unity and determination that gave them strength. Even as they reveled in each other's arms, each touch and shared glance carried the weight of their shared conviction.

They were ready to face whatever darkness awaited them. Together. Or so they thought...

Chapter 7

The first rays of sunlight filtered through the curtains, casting a warm golden glow across Raven's bedroom. Grayson lay beside her, their limbs tangled together, skin still flushed from the night's passion. Raven traced her fingers along the contours of his chiseled jawline, marveling at the raw vulnerability in his piercing eyes.

"Stay with me," she whispered, her voice laced with desire and a hint of vulnerability. The thought of him leaving sent a pang of longing through her chest.

Grayson's lips curved into a tender smile as he leaned closer, pressing a soft kiss on her forehead. "I wish I could, my love," he whispered, his breath warm against her skin. "But I must get back to the estate. Knox is waiting, and there's bourbon to deal with."

Raven sighed but nodded her understanding, pulling Grayson into one final, lingering kiss before they reluctantly untangled themselves from each other's embrace. As Grayson dressed, his movements swift yet graceful, Raven watched him, filled with a mixture of admiration and sadness.

"Until tonight," Grayson promised, his voice low and sensual, as he pressed his lips to her hand. With one last lingering glance, he slipped out of the door, leaving Raven alone with her thoughts. After a while, she finally got up and got dressed.

The sudden sound of a knock on the front door jolted Raven from her reverie, her heart pounding in her chest. Sensing the darkness all around, she grabbed her grandmother's ring, a talisman of protection. She then quickly pulled on the rest of her clothes and hesitantly opened the door, only to find Eva De Young standing there, her porcelain skin and dark hair contrasting sharply against the vibrant morning.

"Didn't expect to see me, did you?" Eva drew, her voice smooth and unnerving as her amber eyes studied Raven intently.

"What do you want, Eva?" Raven asked, her voice laced with suspicion as she instinctively stepped back.

"Grayson," Eva replied simply, a wicked smile curling the corner of her lips. "And I'm not leaving without him."

"Grayson has made his choice," Raven retorted in defiance. "He's not yours to take."

"Is that so?" Eva sneered, taking a step forward, her movements predatory. "You think you can keep him from me?"

"Grayson doesn't belong to anyone but himself," Raven shot back, her voice shaking slightly as she tried to maintain her composure. "He's not some prize to be won and put on a shelf. You cannot just treat him however you want."

"Perhaps not," Eva conceded, her eyes narrowing dangerously. "But you, my dear, are in my way." With lightning-fast reflexes, Eva struck, her hand colliding with Raven's temple. The world around her blurred and darkened as she crumpled to the ground, unconscious.

Eva smirked down at the fallen witch. "I'll be sure to give Grayson your regards," she whispered before hauling Raven's limp body over her shoulder and disappearing into the morning light.

****

Marley and Madison hurried down the cobblestone path leading to Raven's cottage, their heels clicking in rhythm with their pounding hearts. The scent of freshly cut grass mixed with the lingering aroma of last night's bourbon, creating a bittersweet harmony that echoed the urgency in their steps.

"Raven hasn't answered her phone all morning," Marley fretted, her tone filled with worry. "It's not like her to miss work without a word."

"Something isn't right," Madison agreed, her light blue eyes reflecting the same unease. "We will figure it out. She may just be tangled up with Grayson."

As they reached the door, Marley hesitated, her hand hovering over the doorknob. She glanced at Madison, who gave her a reassuring nod. Bracing themselves, they stepped inside, only to be greeted by chaos. Furniture overturned, books scattered across the floor, and there, abandoned on the coffee table, lay Raven's cell phone.

"Mercy..." Marley breathed, her voice trembling as she picked up the phone. "This is bad, Maddie. We need to tell Grayson and Knox right away."

"Let's go," Madison said, her tone laced with determination. "Grayson will lose his mind!"

****

The Beaumont estate loomed in front of them, its grandeur both imposing and comforting all at once. Marley and Madison rushed toward the entrance, their emergency blatant as they ran up the stairs. The door opened as they reached it and hurried inside. Wixx stepped aside, sensing their urgency.

"Grayson! Knox!" Marley called out, her voice echoing through the halls. Within seconds, the brothers appeared, concern etched on their chiseled faces.

"What's happened?" Grayson demanded, his piercing eyes narrowing as he took in the girls' worried expressions.

"Raven's missing," Madison blurted out, her words tumbling over one another. "Her place is a mess, and her phone was left behind."

"Something's happened to her," Marley added, tears welling in her eyes. "We don't know what or who, but we need to find her right *now*."

Grayson and Knox exchanged a brief glance, their shared determination igniting a silent agreement between them. Without hesitation, they sprang into action, tapping into their supernatural senses to locate the missing witch.

"Knox, can you sense her energy?" Grayson asked, his voice tense as he focused on the subtle vibrations of the ley lines beneath their feet.

"Only faintly," Knox replied, his expression clouded with frustration. "But there's something else…a dark presence. It feels like…Eva."

"Damn it," Grayson cursed under his breath. "She must have taken Raven. Let's get in touch with your friend from Salem, see if she can shed some light for us."

Together, the brothers reached out to their witch contact in Salem, using her powers to trace the remnants of Raven's energy and Eva's sinister presence. Moments ticked by, seeming like an eternity, the urgency of the situation growing heavier with each passing moment. Finally, the witch told them where to look, giving them as much detail as her vision would allow.

Raven's life is at stake. I won't let anything happen to her.

With Marley and Madison by their side, Grayson and Knox embarked on a desperate race against time to find Raven and protect her from the darkness that had ensnared her.

The abandoned distillery loomed before Grayson and Knox; its decaying walls shrouded in creeping vines cast ghostly shadows in the overgrown area. The scent of old mold hung heavy in the air, mingling with the unmistakable stench of dark magic that had been used to transport Raven from her home.

"Raven's here," Grayson murmured under his breath, his eyes narrowing with ire as they scanned the crumbling structure. "I can feel it."

"Let's be careful, brother," Knox warned, a flicker of apprehension etched in his tone. "Eva knows we're coming, and she'll be prepared."

As they stealthily approached, Grayson could not help but recall the previous night spent entwined with Raven, their bodies moving together with wild abandon. He could still taste the sweetness of her lips, feel the warmth of her skin against his cold skin. The memory only served to fuel his resolve, igniting a burning desire to save her from the clutches of the malevolent vampire who had taken her from him.

"Grayson," Knox whispered urgently, snapping him out of his reverie. "There she is."

Eva De Young stood in the center of the distillery's main chamber, exuding a sinister elegance that was both alluring and deadly. Her porcelain skin seemed to glow beneath the pale light, while her amber eyes now a sinister red bore into the brothers with chilling intensity.

"Ah, the Beaumont brothers," Eva purred, a wicked smile tugging at her crimson lips. "I've been expecting you."

"Where's Raven?" Grayson growled, his immortal strength surging within him as he fought to keep his emotions in check.

"Patience, my love," Eva taunted, her voice dripping with malice. "You'll find her soon enough."

With a snarl, Grayson lunged at Eva, his powerful frame a blur as he closed the distance between them in mere seconds. But just as their bodies were about to collide, Eva vanished into thin air, reappearing on the other side of the room with a triumphant laugh.

"Is that all you've got?" she mocked, her eyes flashing dangerously.

"Enough games, Eva!" Knox shouted, his own supernatural speed coming into play as he joined Grayson in the attack. Together, they unleashed a barrage of blows upon the elusive vampire, their fists and feet moving with such swiftness that they defied the laws of physics.

Eva fought back with equal ferocity, her vampiric abilities granting her unnatural speed and strength; dark magic surged through her veins, adding to her agility as she dodged their attacks. In one swift movement, she seized Grayson by the throat, her razor-sharp nails digging into his flesh.

"Ah, Grayson," she breathed, her lips brushing against his ear. "I can feel your desire for me. Why fight it?"

"Because you're not the one I want," Grayson spat, his thoughts consumed by Raven's safety as he struggled against Eva's grip. With a surge of adrenaline, he broke free, sending a powerful punch straight into the vampire's jaw.

"Grayson, look!" Knox cried out, pointing toward an open doorway where Raven lay unconscious, her wrists bound in iron chains.

"Raven!" Grayson exclaimed his love for her drowning out the pain from his injuries.

"Get her out of here," Knox ordered, his voice strained as he grappled with Eva. "I'll hold her off."

"Be careful, brother," Grayson warned, before dashing toward his beloved witch with newfound urgency.

Grayson reached Raven's side and began freeing her from her chains, while Knox continued battling Eva, their supernatural powers clashing in a deadly dance of violence and passion.

As Grayson worked on freeing Raven from her chains, she stirred, her emerald eyes fluttering open.

"Grayson," she whispered, the words strained against the chaos. "I can help."

"Raven, you're injured," he replied, as he fumbled with the iron shackles.

"Trust me," she insisted, her gaze unwavering. With a nod, Grayson released her just as Knox stumbled back from a powerful blow delivered by Eva.

Placing her hands on the ground, Raven started speaking in a foreign tongue. Drawing upon the ancient ley lines beneath the distillery, she summoned a protective barrier around herself and Grayson, giving them a momentary reprieve from the battle. Her hands crackled with raw energy, the air around her charged with primitive power.

"Showtime, I guess," Raven muttered, taking a deep breath as she prepared to unleash her full potential.

"Stay close," Grayson warned, his heart racing at the thought of putting Raven in harm's way. But he knew they needed every bit of strength to defeat Eva.

"Always," she promised, her voice laced with determination.

As the barrier dissipated, Raven hurled a torrent of wind at Eva, momentarily distracting her and allowing Knox to regain his footing. Grayson seized the opportunity, a blur of motion as he moved toward Eva, his fists raining down on her in a brutal flurry.

"Give it up, Eva," Grayson growled, his eyes blazing with anger. "You'll never have me."

"Never say never, darling." Eva's wicked smile twisted into a snarl as she countered his attack with her own brutal maneuvers.

Grayson lunged at her, his movements swift and lethal. He landed a powerful punch to her jaw, the impact reverberating in the dusty air. Eva retaliated with a vicious kick, aiming for his midsection. Knox joined the fray, his strikes precise and forceful.

Raven channeled her magic, unleashing a torrent of wind that sent debris flying in all directions. The abandoned distillery trembled under the intensity of their battle. Eva, undeterred, launched herself at Raven with terrifying speed, claws extended.

"Get away from her!" Knox's voice thundered as he shielded Raven from Eva's attack. Grayson roared in defiance, meeting Eva head-on with unyielding strength. The clash of supernatural abilities filled the air with crackling energy.

Eva sneered, her movements fluid and deadly as she attempted to overpower them. But Grayson, Knox, and Raven fought back with unwavering determination and unity. Each strike, each spell cast was a testament to their fierce resolve to protect one another and emerge victorious in the face of darkness.

The battle raged on, echoing through the decaying walls as they clashed in a dance of violence and survival. Every movement, every breath, was infused with urgency and purpose as they battled for their lives.

As the fight escalated, the air grew thick with the scent of aggression, buckets of sweat, and raw bourbon. The decayed distillery had never seen such a spectacle in its lifetime, and its old bones shook with the struggle.

Raven's magic was spreading like wild vines. Green sparks crackled around her fingertips as she summoned earthen spikes from beneath Eva's feet, causing her to lose footing and stumble. Grayson used this chance to strike back hard, sending her sprawling backward onto the musty floorboards.

Knox was a silent storm, his movements fluid and focused as he fought alongside his brother. He landed another powerful blow against Eva, his fist crashing into her like a wrecking ball. The battle echoed off the distillery walls with each hit after hit.

But Eva was not known for surrendering. Rising from the floor, a malicious grin spread across her mouth. With a swift motion of her hand, she sent out a blast of energy that knocked both brothers off their feet and sent them crashing into empty crates that had been left behind.

Heart pounding in her chest, Raven raised her hands toward Eva, chanting an ancient spell under her breath. Thick, green vines snaked around Eva's body, their rough texture scraping against her skin as they bound her wrists and ankles. Seeing Raven's victory, Knox sprang back onto his feet and sprinted toward Eva.

With a roaring shout, he smashed his fists against the vampire with all his might. The impact sent shockwaves throughout the distillery, shattering glass bottles and shaking loose rusted machinery.

Through it all, Grayson watched as Raven stood tall and defiant amidst the chaos. Her hair was wild around her face; her emerald eyes burning with magic. It was not just her supernatural powers that made him fall deeper in love with her; it was her courage, resilience, and unyielding spirit.

Grayson looked over at Knox, and their eyes met for a split second, their unspoken connection fueling their next move. They lunged in tandem toward Eva, catching her off guard as they struck with an enhanced speed only immortals possessed. As they landed their blows, Raven mustered her remaining strength to call upon the raw power of the ley lines beneath their feet.

The ground shook violently, sending shockwaves through the abandoned distillery. The air crackled with electricity as Raven channeled the energy into a force that slammed into Eva, throwing her against the far wall with a thunderous crash.

"Stay down!" Grayson snarled, his voice filled with equal parts, fury and anguish as he watched Eva struggle to rise.

"Eva, I would listen if I were you," Knox growled, standing beside his brother, unwilling to let anything come between them.

For a moment, the world held its breath as Eva lay motionless among the debris. But then, with a final, defeated sigh, she crumbled to the ground, unconscious but alive. Grayson knew it was not over, but they had time. Eva would need to rebuild herself before trying again. He looked out quickly, and when he saw Raven on the ground, panic set in.

"Raven!" Grayson rushed to her side. She lay still, her raven-black hair splayed around her like a halo, her body limp and unconscious. Gently, he cradled her in his arms, his heart breaking at the sight of her so vulnerable.

"Is she…?" Knox trailed off, unable to finish the question.

"Alive," Grayson confirmed, relief washing over him like a wave. "But we need to get her help. That took a lot out of her."

"Marley and Madison are waiting by the road with the car. We will take care of her," Knox reassured.

As they carried Raven out of the crumbling distillery, Knox looked at his brother.

"Grayson, I need to tell you something."

"Go ahead," Grayson replied, his voice weary but attentive.

"During this battle…I realized that I cannot hide my feelings any longer." His voice came out ragged, filled with apprehension. "I have feelings for her. I am sorry, brother. But I promise you, my loyalty to you will always come first. I won't let it come between us."

"Knox," Grayson murmured, torn by his brother's

confession, "we can discuss this later. We are stronger together, remember? And right now, that is what I need. You by my side. Helping me with Raven."

"Absolutely," Knox agreed, his loyalty for his brother unwavering.

As they approached Marley and Madison, the two women rushed forward with worry etched on their faces. The brothers knew that together, they could handle what lay ahead. And as they set about tending to Raven's battered body, their hearts filled with a fierce determination to protect her at all costs.

"Let's take care of our girl." Marley's expression radiated with resolve.

"For sure." Madison nodded, rolling up her sleeves as they all prepared to do whatever to keep Raven safe and their secrets hidden within the shadows of Bourbon County.

Back at the estate, they had prepared a makeshift hospital bed for Raven in the den, taking turns watching over her. Grayson never left her side. Her shallow breaths filled the silence, her chest rising and falling like the ebb and flow of a quiet tide. Her bruised face seemed to glow against the shadows that enveloped them, her raven-black hair fanned out around her like delicate tendrils. Grayson's eyes remained fixated on her, gently caressing her face.

"Grayson, we need to talk about what happened today," Knox said, his deep brown eyes solemn and concerned. "We can't keep hiding who we are."

"Knox is right," Marley chimed in. "If others were near and heard, they will be curious. The supernatural community has always been small here, but they do not like newcomers in the area."

"Y'all have embraced your true selves tonight," Madison added, her gaze darting between the brothers, "but there'll be consequences for those actions. Not sure how others in the area will feel or what the Witch's Council will say."

"Thank you for being here with us," Grayson said, his voice tinged with gratitude. "I know that we owe it to ourselves and each other to confront the risks we have taken and deal with them. I am sure the noise, earthshaking, and lights have attracted us unwanted attention."

"We broke the guidelines, Gray." Knox sighed as he glanced at Raven's unconscious form. "We need to be prepared to face the Witch's Council, and whatever else comes looking for us."

"Then let's make a decision," Raven whispered, her voice weak but determined as she slowly opened her eyes. "You all are not facing any of those challenges without me. We embrace our true selves and protect our secrets. If anyone saw or heard anything, then we deal with it, but together."

"Raven," Grayson breathed, relief washing over him at the sound of her voice. He tightened his grip around her hand, feeling the warmth of her skin. "You're awake."

"Wasn't gonna leave you guys behind," she replied, her lips curling into a faint smile.

As they gathered around Raven, a sense of determination and resolve settled over the group. Grayson looked into the eyes of each person who had come to mean so much to him in such a noticeably short time, knowing that they were stronger together. And with this new family, and his old one by his side, he could step out from the shadows, and for once in his existence…live!

"Whatever lies ahead," Grayson declared, "we will face it as a united front. We will protect our secrets and those we love, no matter the cost."

"Agreed," they all said, their voices united and unwavering.

****

The night was draped in a heavy silence that hung over the estate, the darkness outside punctuated by the soft glow of lanterns. Grayson stood at his window, gazing at the moonlit landscape as he mulled over the events that had unfolded, and what lay ahead for them all.

"Grayson?" Raven's voice called to him from behind, her footsteps barely making a sound on the wooden floor.

"Raven," he replied, turning to face her, concern etched into his features. "You should be resting."

"I couldn't sleep anymore," she admitted, moving closer to him. "I can't help but worry about what's going on in your mind."

"There is no need to ever worry about me," Grayson confessed, taking her hand in his. "Only thing I am thinking about is you." Grayson offered her his best sly smile.

The air between them sparkled with the incandescent electricity they always managed to generate, no matter what the circumstances. Moving closer, she looped an arm around his waist, her body pressing gently against his. "That goes both ways." She tilted her head, looking up at him.

Grayson lowered his head and captured Raven's

lips in a tender kiss. The tension in his body dissolved under her touch as he pulled her closer, muscles relaxing. He found solace in her embrace, the weight that had made its home in his heart easing with every passing second. This, he realized, was where he was meant to be—by her side.

Breaking away from the kiss, Grayson rested his forehead against hers, their breaths mingling in the stillness of the room. "Promise me something," he requested softly.

Raven looked into his eyes. "Anything."

"Promise me," Grayson began, his voice laced with urgency and intensity, "that no matter what happens tomorrow or any day after that...you won't leave my side."

Raven smiled and met his gaze squarely. "I promise," she whispered back. And as she locked her promise into the heart of the man she loved, Raven knew in that moment, this was meant to be, he was meant to be in her life. And nothing, not even an obsessed vampire or a council of witches, could ever change that.

After a few moments, she looked up at him. "Are you afraid?" she asked, her eyes searching his.

"Only of losing those I care about," he responded, his grip tightening around her hand. "But I am more determined than ever to protect it all."

"Good," she whispered, leaning in to place a tender kiss on his lips.

Their shared moment was interrupted by the distant howl of a wolf, its mournful call sending shivers down their spines. They exchanged glances, knowing there were powerful forces at play beyond their comprehension.

"Things are changing," Raven murmured. "I think after all those quite years, Bourbon County is waking up."

"Seems like you are right," Grayson agreed, his gaze drifting back toward the window. "And we must prepare ourselves for all the things that go bump in the night."

****

Unbeknownst to them, Eva De Young lurked in the shadows, her amber eyes glowing with a sinister light. Her body may have been battered and bruised, but her spirit was far from broken. As she watched the lovers embrace through the large window, a twisted smile played upon her lips.

"Enjoy your time together while it lasts," she whispered, her voice filled with malice. "For soon, the darkness will come and claim us all."

With that ominous declaration, Eva vanished into the night, leaving behind only a faint trace of her presence. The winds of change were blowing, and the Beaumont estate would find to be at the heart of a storm that threatened to sweep them away.

****

As Grayson held Raven close, he could not help but feel the weight of responsibility bearing down upon him. So much was happening around them. But the thought that kept pushing forward the most, were Knox's words playing over and over… 'I have feelings for her.' Grayson knew something had been up with Knox. He was hunting more, quiet, moodier even…he just thought it was the reviving the bourbon, that the stress and excitement were getting the better of him.

Grayson had to talk to him, to face what was going on within his brother's mind, but he was worried, and angry, two emotions Grayson hated dealing with, because both caused his immortal side to show.

After Raven fell asleep, Grayson went to look for Knox. It was time to discuss this matter before it drove Grayson crazy.

He found Knox in the courtyard; a glass of their coveted bourbon cradled in his hand as he stood beneath the sprawling branches of an old magnolia tree. His chestnut hair was mussed, and his usually alert eyes seemed lost in thought.

Grayson took a deep breath, allowing the scent of aged liquor mixed with the fragrant undertones of southern jasmine to fill his senses. "We need to talk," he said, his voice echoing in the still, dusk-laden air.

Knox turned toward him, his brown eyes flickering in the encroaching twilight. "About Raven?" His tone gave nothing away, but an unfamiliar knot formed in Grayson's stomach.

"Yes," Grayson said. He paused, searching for the right words. "I know what you're feeling for her. It's more than comfort or friendship…you are in love with her."

Silence engulfed them like a cloak as Knox regarded him with an unreadable expression. Grayson heard the rustle of leaves and from far off an owl hooting solemnly toward the moon. His eyes were on Knox, looking for some reaction. But Knox simply stared at his boots, scuffing them on the ground.

"You don't need to deny it," Grayson continued. "I 've seen how you are around her, protective, and tender. That is usually not you at all."

Then, after what felt like an eternity, he nodded slowly. "I shouldn't have allowed myself, but her charms are so hard to resist. I didn't mean to...I never wanted this."

Clearing his throat Grayson then said, "This is not a confrontation, Knox. I just thought we should...clear things up."

Knox looked away, his gaze landing on the family distillery at the end of the farm. Buying himself time to process the shame he felt for letting his brother down. Without looking at him all he could manage was, "I am deeply sorry, Gray."

Grayson noted the genuine regret in Knox's voice, and it helped to ease some of his inner turmoil. This was not just about him anymore; it never was. It involved all of them—Raven, himself, and Knox.

With a newfound determination surging within him, Grayson steadied himself. He knew this was only the beginning and something deeper was at play— Eva's ominous threats echoing in his mind.

"Remember, brother," Grayson started, "no matter what happens or what feelings we develop or discover...we are family first, and foremost. We cannot let anything ruin that." With these words hanging in the warm Kentucky night air, they both knew things would never be quite the same again.

****

As they were having this important conversation away from prying eyes, Raven was roused from her slumber by a strange sensation. It felt as if something or someone was calling out to her. She rose from the bed, her eyes wide and alert as she moved toward the window. The distant sight of Eva's silhouette made her blood run cold. Realizing what was truly at stake, she knew she had to master her witch powers fast not only for her survival but for the man she had fallen in love with.

In the small hours of the morning, Raven stepped out onto the balcony off Grayson's bedroom, shrouded in a flowing white nightgown that complemented her raven-black hair cascading down around her shoulders. The wind whispered through the trees, the rustle of leaves and distant hoot of an owl providing a haunting soundtrack in the otherwise silent night.

She raised her hands to the sky as she recited an incantation in the blend of Latin and Appalachian dialect passed down by generations of witches in her family. An aura formed around her, the air crackling with energy as she poured every ounce of desire, fear, and determination into mastering her powers.

****

In the Beaumont estate courtyard, Grayson and Knox shared a brotherly moment, lost in their own thoughts as they stared out across the land now cast in shadows. Their heightened senses allowed them to perceive the delicate shift in the air, alerting them to Raven's fervent attempts at unlocking her magic. She was awake, Grayson could feel her.

"This isn't just about us anymore," Grayson murmured, tone etched with concern.

Knox nodded solemnly at his brother's words, feeling a new surge of protectiveness toward Raven.

"Agreed," Knox said gruffly, his chestnut hair tousled by the night breeze. "But we can't let Eva get to her. She's in danger, and that needs to be dealt with once and for all."

Grayson felt a pang at his brother's words, a silent acknowledgment of the invisible thread that now bound all three of them together. He already knew what must be done. He had to confront Eva and get rid of her, no matter what it took.

Suddenly, the peaceful silence of the night was shattered by a piercing scream. Grayson shot upright, his heart pounding in his chest.

Raven.

He vanished in an instant, a shimmering blur of impossible speed that left Knox speechless before he, too, followed with an identical immortal burst of velocity.

Entering his room, Grayson found Raven crumpled on the floor. He reached for her, pulling her close, as Knox and Wixx entered, followed closing by Marley and Madison.

"Raven," Grayson whispered, cradling her unconscious form in his arms. He brushed stray strands of hair from her face, his heart twisting at the sight of her pale features. His gaze flickered to Knox, who stood frozen in the doorway, a whirlwind of worry etched on his face, his jaw clenched tight.

Knox turned away, staring out into the night, the tension in his muscular physique evident. "Eva," he muttered under his breath, then louder to the others in the room, "It has to be Eva playing more games."

Grayson nodded grimly, carefully laying Raven down on the velvet chaise by the room's arched window. He felt a surge of guilt wash over him for leaving her alone. But guilt had no place right now; they needed to act swiftly.

The Beaumont brothers shared a look that carried a

century of shared secrets and unspoken understandings as they looked again out into the night. Raven's safety was their priority, but they also knew the actions they were about to take would have far-reaching consequences for all immortals hiding in plain sight amongst humans. Eva had to be killed.

Raven started to stir. Madison was holding her hand, when Marley said, "Grayson, she's waking up."

In an instant, he was by her side. "What happened? Was it Eva?"

"No, not really here...like a ghost, or memory." Raven, dazed and confused, stumbled over her words as she tried to explain what she'd seen while casting the protection spell around the estate.

"I will get her something to drink, help her to relax," Wixx said as he stepped from the room. The others gathered around her, waiting for more detail.

But Raven's emerald eyes were unfocused, her thoughts still scrambled from the magic she had tried to wield. "I... It was so strong, Grayson," she mumbled, her gaze finally focusing on his face. What she saw there—the tension in his chiseled features, love mingled with fear in his piercing blue-gray eyes—stirred a surge of warmth in her chest.

"Take it easy," he urged, placing a reassuring hand on her shoulder. His touch grounded her, anchoring her to the reality of the high-ceilinged room with its glowing lanterns and flickering shadows. She closed her eyes once again.

As they waited, Raven's eyes fluttered open, a flash of awareness passing through them while she blinked away the haze clouding her vision. "I saw her," she said, her voice hardly above a whisper as Grayson gently brushed his fingers against her cheek. "She was here, but not here."

Grayson shared a look with Knox—they knew what Raven was talking about. Ghostly apparitions were often the work of powerful immortals who had mastered the intricacies of space and time to project themselves into different locations. But how could Eva use such an advanced technique? Did she have a witch helping her? So many questions they needed answers too.

Anger and fear coursed through Knox as he contemplated the possibilities.

Grayson's grip tightened around Raven's hand, his eyes darkening with resolve. This game of cat and mouse Eva orchestrated needed to end, and it needed to end tonight.

Just then, Wixx returned with a steaming mug in his hands, its sweet aroma wafting through the room. He handed it to Raven, who wrapped her hands around the warm, smooth ceramic mug, allowing the heat to chase the chill from her fingers.

Raven managed a small smile at Grayson before turning her attention back to Knox. She recounted how Eva appeared in front of her and taunted her about her relationship with Grayson and the consequences it would have for all of them.

The reality of their situation came crashing down on them—they were up against a vampire with possibly a witch who had experience with dark magic, coupled with Eva's unhealthy obsession. The battle lines had been drawn, and it was clear that they would not emerge unscathed. Raven knew she needed to go to the Witch's Counsil, but with what information. She had no idea if there was another witch, or Eva was on her own.

Their conversation gradually moved from recounting the event to planning for the future. The Beaumont brothers agreed that they had to confront Eva directly—lure her into fate befitting her heinous actions. Eva must die, there was no way around that. And they needed a plan to trap her. To lure her in with no issues.

Grayson stood up facing the window. He watched darkness slowly unfurl over the vast stretch of land their estate covered, the rolling fields cloaked in a mystic shroud. In its quietude, it was easy to forget the storm brewing around them.

Raven broke the silence, "What's the plan?"

Grayson turned around, his eyes gleaming with determination. "We use me as bait," he declared.

Knox's face hardened. "Grayson, that's too risky."

"I know," he admitted. "But it's clear that Eva is after me. If we want to ensure her downfall, I need to be in the picture."

Raven protested fiercely, her voice echoing throughout the room. "I won't let you do this alone. It is not just your fight."

But Grayson was adamant. His gaze locked with hers, a silent plea for understanding as he reached out cupping her face gently. "I cannot risk losing you again, Raven. I will not."

The room fell silent again, everyone grappling with the enormity of what was about to happen. Raven met Grayson's gaze head-on. None of them took it lightly about the idea of ending a life, especially Raven. Witches were supposed to protect, not kill.

"We don't have any other choice, this is our only

way to ensure that she will be trapped," Grayson countered, his eyes pleading with hers.

"He will make good bait, as much as I hate him being alone with her, she's crazy," Knox added softly.

For a moment, only the crackling of the fire filled the room as they waited for her response. She did not like this plan, not at all. But deep down inside she knew they were right; Eva wanted her out of the way so that she could have Grayson for herself.

Finally, she gave a curt nod and sighed deeply. "All right," she murmured, "we'll do it your way. But I will be involved also. I am the only one among us who can truly stand up to her power if there is another witch helping her."

A sense of dread filled them as they began planning their assault against Eva. The stakes were higher than ever before; failure was not an option—too much was at risk.

And as dawn broke over Bourbon County, a new day began, fraught with the anticipation of the deadly confrontation to come. The past and future seemed to collide in this moment, emboldening them for a showdown. Only fate could determine what lay beyond.

Chapter 8

Grayson stood by the window of his study, the vestiges of sunlight casting dancing shadows across the room. He could feel the weight of the impending confrontation bearing down on him like a crushing embrace. The scent of freshly cut grass wafted through the open window, but it did little to calm his nerves.

"Grayson." Raven's voice was soft as she stepped into the room, her deep emerald eyes searching his face for reassurance. "Are you certain about this?"

"Raven," he began, pulling her close and breathing in the familiar, comforting scent of lavender that clung to her. "This is the only way. Eva has become too dangerous, and we must end this threat before it consumes us all."

Her gaze held a flicker of doubt, but she nodded, her fingers tracing the curve of his jaw. "Promise me you'll be safe."

Grayson captured her hand, pressing a fervent kiss to her palm. "I promise," he whispered against her skin, the intensity of their connection leaving him breathless. "For you, I would walk through the fires of hell unscathed."

"Killing her...it goes against everything I stand for," Raven said, her eyes glossy with unshed tears. "As a nature witch, my job is to protect, not destroy."

"Sometimes, protecting means making difficult

choices," Grayson replied, his own heart heavy with the burden they bore. "But remember, we do this to shield those we care for—including each other."

Raven leaned in, capturing his lips in a tender yet passionate kiss that spoke of the depth of their feelings for one another and the challenges they faced together. As they reluctantly parted, Grayson knew he carried her strength within him, fueling his resolve.

"Let's gather everyone," he said, his voice resolute. "We need to go over the plan one last time."

As Knox, Wixx, Madison, Marley, and Raven assembled in the dimly lit living room, Grayson outlined their strategy once more. "Coordination and secrecy are of utmost importance," he emphasized, his piercing blue-gray eyes meeting each of theirs in turn. "We cannot afford any mistakes or missteps. Our lives—and the balance between worlds—depend on it."

"Raven and I will hide nearby, ready to intervene when the moment is right," Knox added, his deep brown eyes reflecting both wisdom and concern. "But Grayson, you must be cautious not to let your emotions cloud your judgment. Eva is a master manipulator."

"I know," Grayson replied, acknowledging the risk with a nod. "But we have no other choice. I'll do whatever it takes to protect those I love." His gaze locked with Raven's, reinforcing their bond.

"Then we're with you," Wixx said, clapping Grayson on the back. The others reaffirmed their agreement, a united front against the darkness that threatened to engulf them.

"We will be waiting here for whatever else you all need," Marley chimed in.

"Let's put an end to this," Grayson declared,

steeling himself for the battle ahead, his heart a maelstrom of determination, passion, and unwavering love for the woman who had irrevocably changed him.

The inky black sky above seemed to ripple with an undercurrent of anticipation as Grayson, his jaw set and eyes blazing with determination, got out of the car at the Limestone Quarry. The sound of distant hooves on cobblestone, a raven's caw, animals scurrying in underbrush, a haunting melody that echoed through the night.

"Are you prepared for this?" Knox's voice broke through Grayson's thoughts, tinged with concern for his brother.

"Of course," Grayson replied, his tone laced with sarcasm. "What could be more enjoyable than a leisurely stroll through a haunted quarry to confront a homicidal ex-lover?" Though he attempted to maintain a façade of confidence, the disquiet gnawing at the edges of his mind betrayed him.

"Stay focused," Raven whispered, laying a hand on Grayson's arm as they approached their hiding spot near the quarry. Her touch sent a jolt of electricity through him, igniting a fire in his chest that burned away some of the lingering dread. "Remember, we're here to protect you, but only act when the time is right."

"Trust me," Grayson murmured, locking eyes with her. "I'll do whatever it takes to end this threat, not just for my sake, but for all of us." His words were a solemn vow, underscored by the intensity of his gaze.

As Grayson descended into the depths of the quarry, the world around him took on a sinister quality. The shadows seemed to thicken like blood in water, and the air grew colder with each step. He couldn't shake the feeling of being watched, as though unseen eyes were tracking his every move.

The moon cast its cold, silver light on the Limestone Quarry, bathing the jagged rocks and murky water in a haunting glow. Grayson's heart pounded in his chest as he took a deep breath, inhaling the damp, earthy scent that clung to the air. He could feel the power of the ley lines beneath his feet, pulsing with ancient energy—a constant reminder that danger lurked at every turn.

A flicker of movement caught his eye, and he tensed, ready for battle. But it was only a lone raven perched on a nearby tree, it's ebony feathers seamlessly blending with the darkening shadows. The raven watched him with intent.

"Grayson," Eva purred, stepping out from the shadows like a ghost from his past. The sight of her stirred a storm of emotions within him, each one more turbulent than the last. "You've decided to see reason, then?"

"Perhaps," he replied noncommittally, meeting her amber-eyed gaze with a steely determination of his own. "But there are conditions, Eva. You have to change."

"Change how?" she asked, her voice dripping with honeyed venom. She moved closer to him, the flickering moonlight glinting off her porcelain skin and casting dark shadows across her face.

"Your dangerous ways," Grayson said, his voice firm despite the quiver of desire that coursed through his veins. "No more threats, no more violence. If you want to be with me, you have to change."

"Is that all?" Eva whispered, her lips parting ever

so seductively as she spoke against his ear. Her breath was warm, sending shivers down his spine, and he struggled to maintain his composure as her hands traced their way down his chest. "If it means having you, I'll do anything."

"Promise me," Grayson demanded, his voice raw with emotion. He knew he was playing with fire, but he couldn't back down now, not when he knew what that meant.

"I promise," she murmured, pressing her body closer to his. And for a moment, Grayson almost believed her.

As she closed the distance even more between them, Grayson's mind raced. He was playing a very dangerous game, one where the slightest misstep could prove fatal. Yet the seductive sway of Eva's hips and the memory of her touch stirred something within him that was difficult to ignore. All immortals have a high sex drive, and it is easy to get lost in that primal need. Stay focused, he reminded himself, repeating Raven's words like a mantra. *Remember why you're here. Remember who you're fighting for.*

"Let me remind you of how it used to be, our connection, the fire between us," Eva purred.

"Then remind me, Eva," Grayson said, steeling himself against Eva's advances. He would not let her ensnare him again, not when the stakes were so high and the lives of those he loved hung in the balance.

Eva's intoxicating scent filled his nostrils, threatening to cloud his judgment even further. Her hand took his, leading it to the small of her back, pressing herself against him as she leaned in closer. Her lips brushed against his neck, sending a shiver down his spine. As her teeth grazed his skin, he tensed but held his ground. A small bite, to mark him, as she liked to do.

Eva's lips moved toward Grayson's neck again, this time with more urgency. She seemed lost in their dance of seduction, and Grayson felt himself begin to sway.

Hidden among the rocks, Raven clenched her fists in frustration. She could sense the connection between Grayson and Eva, a magnetic pull that threatened to tear them all apart. And although she knew it was all part of the plan, it still stung like a thousand tiny knives. Did he truly care for Eva?

Shards of moonlight pierced the darkness, casting ghostly shadows across the limestone quarry. Grayson's pulse raced as he gazed into Eva's amber eyes, tormented by the knowledge that there would be no turning back once he took this final step.

"Grayson," Eva purred, her voice low and sultry as she reached out to touch his face, "you know you want me."

Then, suddenly, the night air was filled with the echoing sound of a wolf's howl. The sudden interruption pulled Eva away from Grayson's neck. He could see confusion and annoyance crossing her face, a stark contrast to the seductive guise she wore moments before.

Realizing the godsend distraction, Grayson took advantage of her momentary distraction. "Eva—" he began, his hands moving from her waist and gently held her at arm's length.

"What is it?" she asked curtly, her eyes narrowing in suspicion. Her gaze darted around the quarry as if expecting some imminent danger to emerge from the shadows.

A soft whisper echoed through the night air. A ripple of magic swirled around them, invisible to the naked eye but palpable to those tuned to its frequency. Grayson felt a tug at his core as Raven cast out her power, reaching out to Eva.

"I'm sorry," he said quietly, looking directly into Eva's eyes. He watched as recognition dawned in them—realization that she'd been tricked.

He moved swiftly. One hand closed around Eva's wrist while the other shot forward, straight into her chest. Eva gasped, her eyes widening in shock as he pulled his hand back out. In his grasp was her heart, still beating with residual life energy.

She collapsed, her body turning to stone before hitting the ground. Silence fell over the quarry—the only evidence of Eva's existence was the heart in Grayson's hand.

"Raven, Knox, come on," Grayson called, his voice heavy with exhaustion as he tossed Eva's heart aside, shuddering at the gruesome sight.

"Is it done?" Raven asked hesitantly, her voice shaking as she emerged from her hiding spot, followed closely by Knox.

"Yes," Grayson muttered, wiping the crimson stains from his hands onto his jeans.

As they stood over her body, they were silent. The knowledge that they had ended a life weighed heavily upon each of them. Raven was the first to speak up.

"We did what we had to," she said quietly.

Grayson nodded, though he didn't speak, his gaze fixed on Eva's lifeless form. After all she had done—

the pain she had inflicted—it was finally over. A nearby noise caught his attention, the lone raven taking flight into the darkening sky. He knew it was a sign that they had made the right decision. His people believed in omens, and a raven was a symbol of ending and beginning.

With Eva gone, Grayson thought they could finally have their peace. But as he turned to Raven, he saw the distress in her emerald eyes and realized his act with Eva had left a scar on her heart. He felt a pang of guilt; he never intended to hurt her.

They disposed of Eva's body in the depths of the quarry, and once the task was complete, their clothes stained with blood and dirt, the trio wordlessly made their way back to the estate. Relief washed over them as they crossed the threshold, but it was tinged with the bitter taste of guilt and pain.

"Thank God it's over," Madison whispered, embracing Grayson as he stepped inside. Wixx and Marley stood nearby, their faces etched with concern and relief.

"Yeah," Grayson mumbled, his voice heavy with emotion. "But we can never forget what we've done, or the price that was paid."

As his eyes met Raven's, a myriad of unspoken emotions passed between them—pain, love, and a renewed commitment to the future they were fighting for. In that moment, Grayson knew that no matter how dark the path ahead might be, they were bound by an unbreakable bond that transcended the boundaries of mortality and magic.

Raven, her heart beating with a mixture of dread and relief, turned away from the gathering. Leaving

Grayson with everyone, she slipped through a side door that led to the sprawling gardens of the Beaumont estate. She needed solitude, the comforting arms of nature to soothe her troubled mind.

Grayson watched her retreating figure and, after exchanging a knowing look with his brother, followed her out silently. He found her standing at the edge of the reflective pool, her slim frame pale as moonlight against the wisteria draped pergola. The water mirrored her ethereal beauty, rippling softly under the cool breeze that rustled leaves in the nearby trees.

He approached her gently as one would a wounded animal, not wishing to startle her. Standing behind her, he whispered, "Raven."

She turned at his voice, her eyes shimmering with tears she refused to shed. "It's over," she said softly.

"Yes," he agreed, moving to stand by her side. His gaze swept over her face, tracing the delicate arch of her brows, the soft curve of her lips, before settling on those mesmerizing eyes. "It is over."

He cupped her cheek as if to reassure himself she was real and unharmed. He saw her swallow hard and take a deep breath before leaning into his touch. His heart swelled with emotion for this fierce woman who had stared down death for him.

"But this," he continued softly, closing the gap between them. "This is not over." He leaned down to capture her lips in a searing kiss that screamed his devotion to her louder than any words could have.

Raven smiled at him, feeling the warmth spread through her. He made her relax and feel safe in his arms. Something she never knew was missing from her life. "Shall we join everyone else?"

Grayson and Raven returned to the gathering, where everyone was enjoying a bourbon to mark the night. They survived. Despite the weight of their actions, they celebrated in hushed whispers. The clink of glasses was a symphony of triumph that played in the background. Sorrow and joy were two sides of the same coin, and tonight they had to indulge in both.

Marley approached them, with relief flooding her features as she hugged Raven tightly. "I'm glad you're okay," she murmured into Raven's hair. Raven gave her a thin smile, squeezing her back.

As they joined the others, Grayson watched Raven from the corner of his eye. He saw how she was putting on a brave face for everyone else. But he had seen the torment in her eyes and knew the toll this event had taken on her.

Once everyone had settled down, Grayson managed to steal Raven away from the crowd. He could sense her lingering hurt, a sharp pang in his chest that echoed with every beat of his immortal heart.

"Raven," he whispered, his voice tender yet urgent, "I need to talk to you."

She looked up at him with those vibrant eyes, guarded but attentive. They stood in the quiet hallway, the murmurs of their friends fading behind them as Grayson took her hand and led her to the grand library. The scent of aged leather and mahogany filled the air as he closed the heavy doors behind them, enveloping them in a cocoon of privacy.

"Grayson, is everything all right?" Raven asked, concern etched on her delicate features.

He stepped closer, his blue-gray eyes searching hers intently. "I can't begin to express how sorry I am for what happened tonight. It was never my intention to hurt you or make you doubt my feelings. Whatever was said to Eva was to hide my true intent."

Raven's gaze wavered, and she looked away, her fingers absently playing with the charms in her hair. "It's just…seeing you with Eva like that, even knowing it was part of the plan, it stirred something inside me. A fear that maybe there's still a part of you that wanted her."

"Raven Ballard," Grayson said firmly, drawing her close so that their bodies pressed against each other, heat radiating between them. "Listen to me. You are the only woman I want. The only one I have ever truly loved. What I had with Eva was an illusion, a twisted game she played with my emotions. But with you…I've found something real, something transcendent."

Grayson's hands cupped her face, his thumbs tracing the curve of her cheekbones. "I love you, Raven," he whispered, their breath mingling in the charged air between them.

"Show me," she breathed, her eyes locked with his, a silent plea for reassurance.

He guided her to his private quarters, a place she had seen many times before, draped in luxurious sheets of midnight blue velvet and adorned with golden accents. The scent of an unmistakably masculine scent that was distinctly Grayson filled the room.

In the center of the room stood a magnificent canopy bed shaped like an archaic four-poster. Enclosed by semi-sheer drapes illuminated by moonlight filtering through grand windows, it looked like something out of a fairytale.

Grayson's lips crashed into hers, a passionate

storm of desire and devotion. He tasted her, savoring the unique blend of herbs and magic that was distinctly Raven. She moaned into his mouth, her arms wrapping around his neck as he pulled her closer to his body.

He trailed kisses down her throat, ravenous and insistent, each touch leaving a trail of fire on her skin. She arched beneath him, desperate for more, and Grayson obliged, his hands deftly unclasping her dress and letting it pool at her feet.

"Grayson," she gasped, her voice heavy with need.

"Shh," he murmured against her skin, his fingers finding the sensitive bud between her legs and stroking it gently. "Let me show you how much you mean to me."

He could barely contain himself as his eyes traced the outline of her curves. His primal need to claim her, to show her just how much he desired her, was taking over. Every fiber of his being was screaming for release.

Without hesitation, he pressed his body against hers, pinning her against the wall. His hands roamed over her hips, pulling her closer until the hardness of his erection pressed into her. He let out a low growl as he bit her earlobe, sending shivers down her spine.

Her breath hitched as his fingers found their way between her thighs, teasing the edge of her panties. He could feel the heat radiating from her core, and it only fueled his desire. With a quick motion, he ripped her panties off, eliciting a gasp from her lips.

His hands moved to her breasts, squeezing and kneading them through her thin bra. She arched her back, pushing herself further into his touch. Her nipples hardened beneath his fingers, and it was almost too much to bear.

He quickly unbuttoned his pants, freeing himself from the confines of his clothing. He lifted her up, wrapping her legs around his waist, and thrust into her with a ferocity that took her breath away.

She let out a moan as he filled her completely, stretching her to the limits. He started to move, sliding in and out of her with a rhythm that was both punishing and pleasurable. She could feel every inch of him as he hit her G-spot repeatedly.

He leaned in, capturing her mouth in a deep, hungry kiss. She could taste herself on his lips, and it only turned her on more. She ran her hands through his hair, pulling him closer as their bodies moved together in perfect harmony.

He could feel his orgasm building, but he wasn't ready for it to end yet. He reached down, finding her clit with his fingers and rubbing it in tight circles. She cried out, her body trembling as she came undone around him.

The feeling of her tightening around him was too much, and he let himself go, emptying himself inside her with a primal roar. He collapsed against her; their bodies still intertwined as they caught their breath.

They stayed like that for a few moments, basking in the afterglow of their shared release. He pulled back, looking into her eyes with a satisfied smirk. "I hope that showed you just how much I want you," he said, before leaning in for another kiss.

She collapsed onto the bed, spent and satisfied. Grayson moved over to her slowly, taking her all in, every detail of her.

"Stay with me tonight," Grayson whispered into

her hair, his voice thick with emotion.

"Tonight, and always," Raven replied, her voice weak from pleasure, a promise sealed between them like a sacred vow.

Grayson gathered her in his arms once more, kissing her deeply and slowly, promising silent words of love and devotion. Their bodies tangled together in the soft sheets, a sensual dance of passion and intimacy. Grayson traced circles on her bare skin, each touch electrifying her senses further.

Raven responded to his touch with soft sighs, her fingers finding their way to his broad chest. She felt the steady beat of his heart under her hand, a rhythm syncing with her own. His lips found hers again in an unhurried kiss.

He brushed a few loose strands away from her face, his chiseled features softening as he stared at the woman resting in his arms. "Have I mentioned how extraordinarily beautiful you are?" His question floated between them like a whispered secret.

She laughed softly, rolling over to bury her face in his chest while murmuring, "Only every day since we met."

The banter came naturally to them, a comfortable rhythm they had fallen into overtime. Their playful exchanges were coupled with raw emotion and an ever-growing passion that consumed them like intoxicating liquor. Their bond was forged with every touch and heated glance, each moment only cementing their connection further.

Grayson's lips descended onto hers once more, initiating another dance of tongues and tangled limbs. Sparks of pleasure radiated from their point of contact, an undeniable proof of the profound bond they shared. The worries of their world faded into the background; for this stolen moment in time, there was only him and her.

****

The first rays of dawn filtered through the gauzy curtains, casting a warm golden light into the room as she lay tangled in Grayson's embrace. A subtle shift in the room's energy stirred her from her post-coital slumber, and she reluctantly opened her eyes to find a small, sealed envelope embossed with the sigil of the Witch Council that had been slid under the door.

Her heartbeat faster in nervous anticipation as she untangled herself from Grayson's grasp and crossed the room to pick it up. The weight of the envelope felt heavy in her hands, filled with the potential to alter the delicate balance they had managed to create.

Bracing herself, she tore open the seal and pulled out a letter written in elegant script. Even before reading it, she knew it brought news from the council, their response to the events of last night.

"Raven Ballard," the letter began, "you are summoned to appear before the Witch Council to address the consequences of your relationship with Grayson Beaumont and the events surrounding Eva De Young's demise. Your presence is required at sundown, three days hence."

"Damn," Raven muttered, feeling a chill run down her spine despite the warmth of the room. She turned to Grayson, who had risen from the bed and now stood beside her, concern etching lines across his handsome face.

"What does it say?" he asked, his voice tight with

worry.

"I've been summoned to the Witch Council," Raven replied, her words heavy with dread. "They want to discuss what happened with Eva and...us."

"Then we'll go together," Grayson said, his grip on her shoulder firm and reassuring. "Whatever they have to say, we'll deal with it."

His words gave her a profound sense of relief, a lifeline in the storm of uncertainty.

"We?" She looked up at him.

"Yes," Grayson affirmed with a determined nod, his piercing gaze unwavering. "We are in this together, Raven. Always."

They stood there for a while, wrapped in each other's arms as if drawing strength from the warmth of the other's body. The letter lay forgotten on the table as they lost themselves in a moment that promised unending solidarity against any adversity that might come their way.

"Let's gather everyone. We need to plan for this," Raven suggested. "We need witnesses."

****

As the group convened in the living room, the air was thick with tension. The glow of overhead lights illuminated their faces, still dark waves wove through that seemed to dance in time with their hushed whispers. Raven recounted the contents of the letter, watching as her friends absorbed the news, expressions of resolve and concern etching themselves onto their features.

Knox was the first to speak, his face serious. "This is expected, in light of the events. We took a life, which is against their nature. And, you both swore to keep a low-profile. They would want to hear from you both."

Raven nodded, her fingers tracing the edges of the letter absentmindedly. The room lapsed into silence, everyone deep in thought, until Marley piped up.

"We will be there with you." She said her tone firm and unwavering. "They need to see that you have support and we can be your witnesses."

"What do you think they will do?" Madison asked, taking in the face around her. The question suspended in the air like a specter.

"It's hard to predict," Raven sighed, "but they must uphold their laws. Our relationship... it is not just frowned upon, it's forbidden. They were giving us a chance to prove we were different, that there would be no killing, no attention of any kind brought to our world. We failed."

"But they can't separate you," Marley protested. "Grayson isn't... he didn't ask for this to happen. Eva caused it. He isn't a monster."

"We should hoe they see reason," Raven stated, her voice calm despite the turmoil that surely roiled within her. "But we must also prepare for them to hold firm to antiquated beliefs."

"Whatever the Witch Council decides," Grayson stated, his eyes never leaving Raven's, "we'll find a way through it."

"Damn straight," Knox agreed, his eyes reflecting the firelight of the fireplace as he clenched his fists in solidarity.

"Besides, who are they to judge us?" Marley drawled defiantly. "You did what you had to do."

"True," Raven admitted, her voice tinged with uncertainty. "But they wield considerable power, and we cannot afford to underestimate them."

"Raven's right," Madison chimed in, her usually bubbly demeanor subdued. "We must face the council with humility and respect. If we come off as defensive or combative, it will only make matters worse."

"Then let's prepare ourselves accordingly," Grayson suggested, his tone resolute. "We'll stand by you, Raven, no matter what the outcome."

"Thank you," Raven whispered, her heart swelling with gratitude and love for the friends who had become her family. As they huddled together, their faces a tableau of determination and solidarity, she knew that whatever the Witch Council threw at them, they would face it head-on.

"Raven," Grayson murmured, his strong arms enveloping her from behind as he pressed his body against hers. His hot breath tickled her ear, sending shivers down her spine. "There's no use in worrying anymore today. We've done all we can right now."

"Easy for you to say," she retorted, her voice soft yet laced with anxiety. "Your fate isn't hanging in the balance. They could also take away my powers."

"I won't let them punish you for my actions," Grayson insisted, his fingers tracing delicate circles on her waist. "We're in this together, remember?"

"Of course." Raven allowed herself a small smile as she leaned into his embrace, finding solace in his unwavering support. But beneath her calm demeanor, a storm of emotions raged within her: fear, doubt, and a fierce determination to protect what they had built together.

"I will take full responsibility for what happen to Eva. You are not alone. We will see you through."

Grayson smiled at her as he tried to reassure her.

"Whatever happens," Knox interjected, his voice tinged with concern as he approached the pair, "we'll be beside you every step of the way."

"Thank you." Raven turned to face him, her gaze meeting his resolute expression. In that moment, she knew the bond they shared transcended any obstacles they might encounter.

"All right," Marley chimed in, her voice breaking the solemn silence. "Enough with the pep talks. Let's get some food. We have a few big days in front of us. Remember, we also have bourbon to get bottled and ready to go out."

As they made their way to the kitchen, Raven couldn't help but feel the weight of uncertainty bearing down upon her. The day was charged with tension, each rustle of leaves or the distant hoot of an owl amplifying her unease. But as she stepped through the estate, the familiar warmth of the manor enveloped her like a comforting embrace.

Amidst the uncertainty, the manor was a beacon of solace, the scent of aged leather and smoky oak lingering in the air, a testament to its deep-rooted history and resilience. The estate had weathered dark times before. It would weather this storm too.

****

After a long day of work mixed with worry and comforting words, Raven found herself alone in Grayson's bedroom, her heart heavy with the looming summons. She sat on the edge of the bed, her gaze fixed on the ornate carvings etched into the wooden bedpost. Her mind wandered to the day she first met Grayson, full of charm and charisma that instantly drew her to him.

"Are you okay?" Grayson's voice was a soft rumble as he entered the quiet room.

"I don't know," she admitted with a sigh. She could hear him moving around in the darkness before his hands found her waist, and he pulled her back against him.

"We'll get through this," he whispered against her hair softly before leaving hot kisses down her bare shoulder. His husky voice and steady embrace were a welcome distraction from her racing thoughts.

Grayson's touch ignited an electric charge that coursed through Raven's veins, grounding her amidst the chaos. She turned around to face him, finding comfort in his solid presence. Her fingers traced along his chiseled jawline, highlighting every perfect angle of his face under the dim light filtering through the blinds.

"You're right." She sighed, pressing herself closer to him.

Their lips met in a feverish kiss, their tongues battling for dominance. The world outside ceased to exist as they lost themselves in each other, the taste and touch of Grayson consuming Raven's senses. This moment of intimacy was a stark reminder of what was at stake—their love, their bond—it was all worth fighting for.

Grayson lifted her effortlessly, his arms wrapping tightly around her waist as he pinned her against the bed. She gasped in surprise, her fingers tangling within his dark locks as he traced a path down her throat with his lips. Her heart thudded wildly in her chest, each beat echoing Grayson's name.

"I love you," Grayson murmured between stolen

breaths, the heat of his gaze searing into Raven's soul.

His words unraveled her completely, melting away her fears. In that moment, all that mattered was him and the intoxicating spell he had cast over her heart.

"And I love you," she whispered back, wrapping her arms around him tighter.

He pushed himself up onto his elbows, his gaze locked onto hers as he slid his hands down her body. His fingers traced the curve of her hip, teasing the sensitive flesh just above her thigh. She gasped, her back arching as he dipped his head to capture her nipple between his lips. The sensation sent a jolt of pleasure straight to her core, causing her to buck her hips against him.

He groaned, the vibration of his voice sending shivers down her spine. He explored every inch of her with reverent touches. His rough hands skimmed over the sensitive skin of her belly, making her squirm with anticipation. Raven let out a soft moan, her fingers clutching his broad shoulders, the hard muscles beneath his skin flexing with each movement.

"Grayson..." she murmured, her voice barely above a whisper as she surrendered to the onslaught of sensations he was eliciting. The desire in his eyes was palpable, a mirror to the want and need coursing through her veins.

"I'm here, Raven," he whispered against her skin, his breath hot and tantalizing. His fingers traced her inner thighs, teasingly close to where she needed him most.

"Please," she whimpered, desperation lacing her voice as she lifted her hips in a silent plea. Grayson gave a low growl in response, his icy gaze never leaving hers as he moved to answer her need.

The world outside ceased to exist as they became lost in their shared desire. The intensity of it all was overwhelming yet breathtakingly beautiful—a testament to their unyielding bond. Their bodies moved together in perfect harmony, each crest and fall echoing their intimate connection.

After their climax ebbed away, leaving them spent and panting, Grayson held Raven close against his chest. His heartbeat steadily beneath her ear—a comforting rhythm that lulled her into contentment. She traced lazy patterns on his sweat-dampened skin, savoring the closeness they so desired and fought to keep.

As Raven lay in the darkness, her thoughts swirling with anticipation and dread, she couldn't help but wonder what this week would bring. Would the Witch Council show mercy, or would they sever her connection to the life she had built with Grayson and their friends? Despite her fears, one thing remained certain: whatever challenges awaited them, she would face them head-on, bolstered by the love and loyalty of those who stood beside her.

When sleep finally claimed her, Raven's dreams filled with visions of moonlit gardens, the scent of blooming magnolias, and the taste of forbidden love on Grayson's lips, a promise of passion and devotion that transcended even the darkest of shadows.

Chapter 9

The sun was rising in the sky, riding the shadows from across the rolling hills of central Kentucky as Raven stood alone in her small cottage deep within the woods. She closed her eyes and took a deep breath, inhaling the earthy scent of damp soil mingled with the faint aroma of wildflowers carried on the morning breeze.

"Focus," she whispered to herself, drawing energy from the ancient ley lines that coursed beneath her feet. She needed clarity before the council meeting, where she would have to defend not only her relationship with Grayson but also what they had done to Eva.

Inhale and exhale—the rhythm of her breaths synced with the steady heartbeat of the earth. With each breath, her anxieties began to melt away, replaced by quiet determination. Raven mentally rehearsed her arguments, seeking the words that might convince the council to let her, and Grayson continue their forbidden love.

"Raven," a familiar voice called out, jolting her from her meditative state. It was Madison, her lifelong friend and confidante, who approached with an expression of concern etched upon her face. "I just received word from the council. They've requested the presence of Grayson and Knox at the meeting."

Raven's heart skipped a beat. On the one hand,

relief washed over her at the prospect of Grayson being there to speak for himself, with the council's permission. But alongside that relief came a wave of apprehension. If the Immortal brothers were to attend, it meant that the council was considering matters far beyond just her relationship with Grayson. The events involving Eva and the dark magic she was thought to have brought into the supernatural balance in Bourbon County into question. Raven had no real proof of what Eva was doing, but she had felt it deep within her.

"Thank you for letting me know, Madison," Raven replied, her voice betraying a hint of the turmoil roiling within her. Her gaze flickered back to the twilight-dappled forest around them. "I suppose it's better they're there to give their side of the story, but I can't help feeling like we're walking into a lion's den."

"Sometimes, facing the lions has to be done," Madison offered, placing a reassuring hand on Raven's shoulder. "No matter what happens, remember that you are not alone. We'll all stand with you. You all had no choice; she would have destroyed us all."

As the shadows disappeared and the murmurs of the forest grew softer, Raven steeled herself for the challenges ahead. No matter what the outcome, she would do whatever it took to preserve her love and defend what they had done.

****

The sun dipped below the horizon, casting a deep crimson glow across the sky as Raven stood on the edge of the farm. She took a deep breath, clearing her mind and filling her senses. Her heart raced, the anticipation of the night's events taking root in her chest.

"Everyone, please," she called out, beckoning

Grayson, Knox, Marley, and Madison to gather around her. The group formed a close-knit circle, their expressions etched with worry and determination. The air between them crackled with tension, the weight of what was at stake heavy upon each of them.

"Thank you for coming," Raven began, her voice wavering slightly. "I wanted us to discuss the possible outcomes of tonight's council meeting. We need to be prepared for anything."

Grayson reached for her hand, his touch comforting and warm. His blue-gray eyes bore into hers, offering strength and support. "It will work out fine, Raven. Just have a little faith in it."

Raven nodded, grateful for the reassurance but still unable to shake the underlying fear that threatened to unravel her. She glanced at each of her friends, their faces illuminated by the flickering light of the nearby fire pit. "My greatest concern is losing my magic—and losing Grayson. If the council decides our relationship is too dangerous to the balance of nature, I don't know what I'll do." Her voice broke, betraying her vulnerability.

"You won't lose either," Marley insisted, her tone fierce and unwavering. "You're one of the most powerful witches I've ever known, and your bond with Grayson is undeniable. Together, we'll make the council see that."

"Marley's right," added Madison. "We'll stand by you every step of the way. What transpired was not your fault. You did not break any of their codes."

"Grayson and I have seen much in our immortal lives," Knox said, "but one thing remains constant: love is a force to be reckoned with. We got this! We will walk away with no issues."

Raven felt the knot in her chest loosen ever so slightly, their words providing a sliver of hope amid the uncertainty that lay ahead. Her eyes met Grayson's once more, their connection electric and undeniable.

"Thank you," she whispered, her voice low. "Your support means everything to me."

Grayson leaned in, his lips brushing against her ear as he whispered, "We'll get through this, Raven. Together, we are unstoppable."

The waning crescent moon pierced through the canopy of tangled branches overhead, casting an eerie glow on the forest floor as Raven led her companions through the gnarled roots and underbrush. The air was electric with tension, charged like the calm before a violent thunderstorm.

"Here," Raven whispered, as they entered the secluded glade. The heady scents of ancient magic filled her nostrils, making her stomach knot in anticipation. Despite knowing in her heart that she was innocent, a gnawing guilt, like a persistent claw, raked across her soul.

The elder witches sat encircled, their ebony robes melding with the shadows encasing them. Their faces were hard and unmoving, as if chiseled from the stones beneath them. Even the flickering candle flames surrounding the witches hesitated, wary of intruding upon their grave deliberations.

"Raven Ballard," intoned the head crone, her voice a rasping echo that sent shivers down Raven's spine, "you have brought your plea to this council. Present yourselves."

"Thank you, Elders," Raven replied, stepping

forward, her gaze fixed on the impassive visages of the witches. Grayson, Knox, Marley, and Madison followed, standing united beside her.

As they stood before the scrutinizing elders, Raven could feel their piercing stares like a crushing weight, their probing gazes seeming to peel back her soul's layers. She fought to maintain her composure, digging deep for strength she never knew she possessed.

Let them see the truth, she thought, steeling herself for the interrogation to come. *Let them understand our love is worth fighting for. And that Eva posed a dire threat to them and the town.*

"Very well," the head crone continued, her steely gaze never leaving Raven's face. "We will hear your arguments, then make our ruling. Remember, our decision will be absolute."

"Understood," Raven replied softly. Each word was a battle, but she refused to surrender to fear.

"Then let us commence," the elder witch declared, setting in motion the council meeting that would decide the fate of Raven's love for Grayson—and their interwoven destinies.

As Raven stood before the council, a wave of anxiety washed over her. Her heart pounded in her chest, each beat echoing the fear she held for the council's judgment. She knew her relationship with Grayson, an immortal, was forbidden by their laws, but she was determined to defend their love.

The head witch, with a cold, measured voice, asked Raven to justify why their relationship should be allowed to continue. Raven took a deep breath, her voice steady, as she replied, "Our love is pure and true. It transcends any law or boundary. We understand the risks and are willing to face them together."

Grayson, standing beside her, met the elder's gaze, his eyes filled with determination. He acknowledged the potential dangers their relationship posed to the magical community, but remained optimistic that their love could bring about change and understanding between the mortal and immortal worlds.

Knox then stepped forward and recounted his encounters with Eva, and the possible witch they think who had manipulated events to drive a wedge between Raven and Grayson. His voice trembled with anger as he spoke of Eva's malicious intentions, but he remained unwavering in his support for his brother's love.

Marley and Madison shared their experiences with Eva and the dark powers she seemed to be connected to. They recounted the harrowing brush with death as they fought to protect each other, and they emphasized the importance of Raven and Grayson's love in their lives.

As each person shared their experience, the tension in the grove grew thicker, suffocating in its intensity.

The head witch stood, speaking in ancient tones. "Tonight, we have heard truths hidden and fears laid bare," she began solemnly. "We were aware of dark magic penetrating our land, though the source remained hidden due to a powerful veil shielding it. No Eva did not act alone. The council will investigate this thoroughly. We also recommend you all refrain from meddling until we conclude that."

She then turned back to her fellow council members, then the council of elder witches retreated to deliberate on the evidence presented before them. In the meantime, a silence settled over the grove, the only sound the soft rustling of leaves under a cool night breeze. The fate of Raven and Grayson, as well as their friends, now rested in the hands of the council.

Inside the circle, Grayson reached for Raven's hand, intertwining their fingers. He looked into her eyes, a silent vow passing between them. Knox offered a nod of support, an unspoken solidarity radiating from him.

Raven's heart raced as the council retreated. Her body trembling despite her efforts to remain composed. She clenched one fist at her side her frustration getting the best of her in this moment of uncertainty.

"Whatever happens," Grayson whispered into her ear, his breath hot against her skin, "I'll always love you." His words were both a promise and a seduction, a reminder of their passion and a testament to their resolve.

"I will love you forever," Raven replied softly, her gaze locked on him. The weight of anticipation pressed down upon them like an invisible hand, suffocating their very beings.

As they waited, time seemed to slow to a crawl, each second stretching out into an eternity. Cold sweat formed on Raven's brows, her breath coming in shallow gasps as anxiety built. But through it all, Grayson's presence served as her anchor, a constant reminder of the love that had brought them to this point.

As the council of witches huddled together in the distance in quiet discussion, their whispers were carried away by the wind, leaving Raven and her companions in agonizing suspense. A palpable tension hung in the air, thick and heavy, with a mixture of anticipation and fear. The moon's glow seeped through the canopy of trees overhead, casting an ethereal radiance over the clearing.

Underneath the weight of the silence, Raven's heart throbbed against her chest. She squeezed Grayson's hand in return, grounding herself in his solid presence. Silence reigned as time stretched on, turning seconds into agonizing minutes. An owl hooted somewhere in the darkness, its voice echoing across the vast emptiness.

Raven's chest tightened with each breath, her gaze constantly shifting between one elder witch to the next as they came back into view. Their disguised expressions only heightening the tension that hung heavily in the air.

"Raven." Grayson's free hand brushed a strained of hair from her face, a gentle reminder of the passion they shared. "Whatever they decide, nothing can take away what we have."

"Grayson," she whispered, her voice shaking like leaves caught in a gentle breeze. "I can't bear the thought of losing you...or my magic."

"Stay strong, Raven," he replied, blue-gray eyes burning with determination.

Finally, after what felt like an eternity, the elder witches returned to their seats. Their faces were impassive as they looked upon Raven and Grayson, their eyes glinting under the glow of countless stars above them. "We have reached a decision," the head crone announced.

A chill cascaded through Raven as she braced herself for whatever was to come. She kept her gaze steady as she looked at each member of the council, attempting to read any hint of their decision from their inscrutable expressions.

Her breath hitched as the head witch spoke again. "We find no treachery in your intentions," she said while looking around at everyone. "We believe your connection is pure. And as for the dark magic, like we stated before, we will investigate further."

A wave of relief replaced the suffocating tension that had gripped Raven, a gasp escaping her lips. Grayson held her closer.

"However," she continued, silencing any premature celebrations, "we cannot ignore the risks. The laws forbidding relationships between witches and Immortals exist for a reason. Raven, you have immense powers, but you are still part human. You will age, and one day return to nature. Grayson is Immortal, therefore he could live forever...will he uphold our laws and protect our secrets forever?"

Raven swallowed hard. She was finding it difficult not to flinch at the truth.

The younger of the council spoke, "You must be careful not to expose our world to mortal eyes."

Raven nodded, ignoring the knot forming in her stomach.

The elder witch declared, "Thus..." She paused, taking another look at the group, then continued. "We here by permit this relationship on a few conditions. That you both swear on your magic and immortality to protect our covenant, to guard our secrets fiercely and ensure the safety of our realms, no attention brought to us, as long as either of you roam these worlds."

"We swear it," Raven said, as Grayson just nodded in agreement.

The council also decreed that Eva's dark magic

will be vanquished and purged from their land, for them not to worry A collective sigh of relief rippled through the grove—a tangible release of tension.

"Lastly," said the elder witch, "we are keeping an eye on you...all of you." Her gaze swept over them before settling back on Raven and Grayson. "The balance between our worlds is delicate. Even love cannot override our duty to protect it."

Raven understood the warning underlying those words—they were on probation. But at least they were together and free...for now.

As the last words of the council dissipated into the cool night air, Grayson turned toward Raven. Staring at her with a twinkle in his eyes, he whispered fervently, "We made it."

"Yes," she whispered back, her voice barely audible as tears shimmered in her eyes. "Yes, we did." She leaned onto him, capturing his lips with a searing kiss that held their shared relief, love, and determination to face an uncertain future together. Their friends looked on, sharing their triumphant moment, knowing they had traversed through the eye of the storm, bracing themselves for whatever came next.

With the setting of new rules and guidelines by the council, Raven and Grayson's forbidden love had been acknowledged and allowed to continue—a beacon of hope despite the darkness surrounding them. Their destinies were now irrevocably intertwined, their love story a testament to the power of love defying all odds.

The elation that radiated from Raven and Grayson's linked hands created an electric current, a tangible connection that seemed to defy the stern gazes surrounding them. Knox, Marley, and Madison, who had been holding their breaths through the entire ordeal, finally released sighs of relief, their shoulders relaxing as they exchanged tentative smiles.

"Thank you," Raven murmured to the council, her voice trembling but laced with gratitude. She met each elder witch's gaze, acknowledging the weight of their decision and silently vowing to honor their agreement.

"Remember," the head witch warned, her eyes fixed on Raven, "the balance is fragile. Do not take this opportunity for granted, or it may be taken away just as swiftly."

As the council members dispersed, returning to their individual paths in the woods, Raven turned to face Grayson. The moonlight filtered through the treetops, casting shadows across his strong features and making his piercing eyes seem even more enigmatic than usual.

"Gray," she whispered, reaching up to trace the curve of his jaw, "we did it. We're together, despite everything."

His fingers entwined with hers, grounding her in the moment. "Yes," he breathed, his voice a rich, velvety timbre. "We've been given a chance, and I won't let anything jeopardize that."

Raven's heart swelled with emotion, her eyes shimmering with unshed tears. They stood there, wrapped in each other's arms, savoring the victory that tasted both sweet and bitter on their tongues. For now, they were allowed to love openly, but the future loomed like an unknown shadow lurking just beyond the edge of their vision.

Turning away from the now deserted spot where the council had convened, Raven led their group back toward the Beaumont estate. The looming trees rustled in the night, whispering secrets to the moonlight as it filtered through, casting an ethereal glow around them.

Once they were safely ensconced within the walls of their haven, the five friends collapsed into the worn leather sofas of the great room, exhaustion seeping into their bones. Grayson's arm encircled Raven securely as she nestled into his side, her head on his chest. His steady heartbeat thumping beneath her ear was a soothing rhythm that lulled her weary mind.

Knox poured generous servings of bourbon into crystal tumblers, passing them around as they collectively exhaled, a toast to their hard-fought victory and to the challenges that lay ahead.

Madison broke the silence first. "We've got a tough road ahead of us," she said softly, her gaze resolute as she held up her tumbler. "But we've faced worse. And we've come out stronger each time."

Raven watched as Grayson clinked his glass against hers before turning toward her, his eyes burning with fierce determination. "To us."

"To us," Raven echoed back softly. Her heart pounded wildly against her rib cage as she savored the taste of bourbon on his lips when he leaned down to claim another searing kiss from her.

As their lips melded together in a passionate dance of love and yearning, the taste of victory was sweet on their tongues. The echo of the council's stern warning still hung heavy in the air, a reminder of what they risked.

Their love story, intertwined with darkness and light, hope and despair, had been etched into the fabric of their existence. As Raven fell asleep in Grayson's arms that night, her dreams were filled with images of their shared past, present, and an undefined future. Her last waking thought was of them standing together on a precipice overlooking a sea of uncharted challenges, ready to dive in hand-in-hand. Their love was a beacon that illuminated even the darkest corners.

Their destinies had been sealed tonight by a council of ancient witches under the watchful eyes of the Kentucky moon.

Grayson gently brushed a loose strand of hair away from Raven's face as she slept, her breathing steady and rhythmic in the quiet room. He was awash with a myriad of emotions—relief, elation, wariness—but mostly an overwhelming sense of love for the woman cradled in his arms. His eyes traced the delicate lines of her face, lingering on those striking emerald eyes now concealed beneath heavy lids. Even in sleep, she was resplendent.

Meanwhile, Knox paced in his study, nursing a glass of bourbon as he pondered their situation. The council may have temporarily assuaged them, but he knew better than anyone that its magnanimity was fickle. A myriad of questions plagued his mind—Who else was involved with Eva? What vulnerabilities had the dark witch exploited?

The rustle of paper drew his attention toward the large oak desk where he'd been meticulously deciphering ancient texts that chronicled ley lines and immortality. Among the scattered parchments lay a small leather-bound journal. It was an heirloom passed down through generations of Beaumonts, filled with century-old secrets and wisdom. Knox knew that within these pages might lie their salvation or their downfall.

As moonlight streamed through the arched windows, dancing shadows across the room's antique furnishings, Knox took a moment to take stock—their existence had just become exponentially more complex. But they weren't alone in this battle; they had each other.

Back in the great room, Grayson had carried a still sleeping Raven up to their shared bedroom. He gently laid her on their bed and covered her with a blanket embroidered with subtle sigils of protection.

As Marley and Madison retreated to their temporary respective quarters in the expansive mansion, they exchanged meaningful glances; a silent communication borne from the trials and shared experiences. Despite the sense of relief, they both knew they were standing at the threshold of unprecedented challenges.

As the night deepened, the Beaumont estate fell into the kind of hushed silence that only the late hours could bring. Despite the uncertainty looming over them, there was still a sense of peace, a shared understanding that whatever battles lay ahead were to be fought together.

Grayson retired to the balcony overlooking their sprawling estate. As he looked out at the moonlit expanse, his thoughts meandered back to Raven. The immense love he felt for her filled him with a profound sense of purpose.

He would do everything in his power to protect her and their love from any threat. Grayson knew now more than ever that he wasn't just battling for his love but for his existence, their existence. With this resolve burning within him like an undying flame, he retreated into their shared space, where Raven was softly breathing in deep slumber.

****

The following morning, Raven woke to the comforting scent of freshly brewed coffee wafting through the grand halls of the Beaumont estate. Grayson, still peacefully asleep with his arm thrown possessively over her waist, was a stubborn reminder of the night's victory. Raven allowed herself a moment of indulgence, memorizing the way his dark lashes fanned out over his high cheekbones, how his breath stirred the loose tendrils of hair resting against her neck. The tension from the previous evening seemed to have ebbed away, leaving only warmth and an unspoken promise resonating in the silence of their shared space.

Careful not to rouse him, she slid out from under his arm and padded silently out of the room, she headed to the kitchen. As she poured herself a mug of coffee, her thoughts swirled around the events that had transpired at the council meeting. The echo of their stern voices lingered in her mind, reminding her of the fragile peace they had achieved and the looming uncertainty they faced.

Yet as she sipped from her mug, warmed by the familiarity of it all, a sense of calm washed over her. She felt strangely invincible standing in Grayson's kitchen, under the silent watch of Knox's oil portrait on the wall, fortified by Madison's and Marley's unwavering support.

Grayson finally joined her in the kitchen just as dawn was breaking over the undulating Kentucky countryside. The cool morning light accentuated his chiseled features, making him look nothing less than divine. His sleepy grin when he caught sight of Raven sent electricity coursing through her veins.

"Good morning," he murmured against her neck, wrapping his arms around her waist and pulling her close. His signature scent of a hint of sandalwood blended with remnants of last night's cologne invaded her senses, causing a heady warmth to bloom within her chest.

"Good morning," she replied, leaning back into his embrace as the heat from his body seeped through her thin robe. The intensity of his piercing gaze woke every nerve in her body with his silent promise. It was a promise that despite the inevitable challenges and potential threats looming on their horizon, he was unwavering in his commitment to protect their love.

As the day wore on, the Beaumont estate buzzed with an undercurrent of anticipation, for what they did not know. But, none the less they were thankful to be here together, and content to search for a normal life that they all craved.

Knox found himself in the rustic charm of his distillery, the scent of aging bourbon acting as a familiar comfort. It was here, amidst the barrels, that he found solace from the weight of the world. His keen eyes were drawn to the golden liquid sloshing gently within the clear glass decanter, reflecting the scattered sunlight that filtered through the dusty windows.

His mind wandered to Raven, her determined spirit and fiery resolve. He admired her strength, her ability to face fear and uncertainty with grace. Yet with their newfound freedom came an undercurrent of danger. A dark magic had been awakened, no doubt about that. Eva did not act alone. It had to have been an ominous force that urged the council to place a warning not to get involved. His mind turned with the knowledge the witches knew more then they were saying. He felt it to his core. And he be damned if he ignored that. The thought of any harm coming to Raven weighed heavily on his heart. He knew he would do whatever it took to protect her...*them*.

****

In the days that followed, Raven and Grayson adapted to their new circumstances. Her day-to-day routine remained much the same—spells to cast, herbs to gather, bourbon to brew. With Marley and Madison by her side, she poured herself into work, then at night was always by Grayson's side.

Grayson, on the other hand, found himself grappling with a restlessness that had not been there before. He filled his days with tasks around the estate, working on the bourbon with Knox and seeing to their lands. His nights, however, were consumed with thoughts of protecting Raven and keeping his new family safe. Despite these worries gnawing at his peace, he couldn't help but relish in stolen moments with Raven—mornings filled with hushed whispers and evenings dotted with passion.

Knox retained his stoic demeanor throughout it all, pouring his focus into the meticulous art of bourbon-making, and keeping his thoughts about the council to himself. It was a meditative process for him, each step brimming with purpose and a quiet intensity. These hours alone in the distillery allowed him time to digest recent events and strategize his next steps.

As for the Beaumont estate itself, it seemed almost untouched by their precarious situation. Its grandeur remained unscathed. It simply bore witness to the secrets, bourbon, and love that unfolded within its walls.

****

One evening, under the indigo sky embroidered with pinpricks of twinkling stars, Raven found herself standing on the edge of a small pond on the estate. Its surface was as smooth as glass, reflecting the night sky. She allowed her witch senses to reach out, feeling the thrum of energy from the ancient ley lines beneath the ground.

As she stood there, lost in the rhythm of nature and magic, a pair of strong arms slipped around her waist. Grayson's voice, a comforting rumble behind her, whispered, "What do you feel?"

"Everything," she replied, resting her hands atop his. "The energy of this land, its magic...it's almost overwhelming."

"Is it too much?" he asked, concerned lacing his words.

"No." She smiled. "It's like a heartbeat, strong and steady. It feels like...like home."

He pressed a gentle kiss to her neck, his voice warm as he murmured against her skin, "As long as I am with you, Raven Ballard, anywhere can be home."

Chapter 10

Grayson methodically measured out several glasses of bourbon. The scent of freshly cut grass and aging bourbon hung in the air, mingling with the occasional whiff of deep, earthy molasses. Knox stood nearby, his eyes narrowed in concentration as he meticulously inspected a charred oak barrel, ensuring its readiness for their first batch.

"Gray," Knox murmured, his voice laced with old-world charm, "are you certain we've got the proportions right?"

"Trust me, brother," Grayson replied, flashing Knox a confident grin. "We've studied our family's recipe countless times. This will be the finest bourbon that was ever made."

As they worked in harmony, Grayson couldn't help but notice the subtle tension between him and Knox. It didn't hinder their dedication to perfecting the bourbon, but it was present, nonetheless. Despite this, the brothers shared an unspoken understanding that transcended their occasional disagreements, bound together by their mutual passion for the family business.

****

The atmosphere inside the Witch's Brew distillery was entirely different. A warm, inviting energy filled the room, punctuated by the sound of laughter and the

185

clink of glass vials. Raven stood at the center of the space, her eyes twinkling with mischief as she infused their unique batch with magical elements.

"Ready, Marley?" Raven asked, playfully raising an eyebrow.

"Of course, sugar," Marley replied, her Southern accent dripping with charm. She carefully added a few drops of a shimmering liquid into the concoction, causing it to bubble and change color.

"Madison, it's your turn," Raven said, her lips curving into a smile as she handed her friend a delicate, lavender-hued crystal.

"Watch and learn, ladies," Madison teased, her light-blue eyes sparkling with mischief. She dipped the crystal into the bubbling brew, letting it absorb the essence of their creation.

The camaraderie between Raven, Marley, and Madison was recognizable as they worked together, seamlessly incorporating the magical elements that set their bourbon apart from others. Each woman brought her own unique touch to the process, their bond of sisterhood evident in every gesture and shared glance.

"Here's to Witch's Brew," Marley declared, raising a glass filled with their newly-crafted bourbon.

"May our magic enchant every taste bud," Raven added, clinking her glass against Marley's and Madison's.

As they drank, the powerful flavors of their creation danced on their tongues, the magic within it thrumming like an intoxicating heartbeat. The perfect blend of friendship, passion, and mystery had been captured within each drop of their bewitching elixir, setting the stage for a truly unforgettable bourbon review.

****

The moonlight cast a silvery glow over the distillery, where Knox Beaumont stood alone, lost in thought. His eyes traveled over the rows of gleaming copper stills, reflecting on the journey that had brought him to this moment. Grayson and Raven's happiness was undeniable, and as much as it pained him to admit, he couldn't help but feel a sense of relief. It was time for him to focus on his own passions, and that meant creating a bourbon blend unlike any other.

Knox's eyes narrowed with determination as he meticulously measured out ingredients, adjusting their proportions with an artist's precision. The scent of charred oak and caramel filled the air, mingling with the subtle hints of vanilla and spice. He could feel the energy coursing through him, driving him to push the boundaries of bourbon-making even further.

"Ah, there you are, darlin'," a sultry voice murmured from behind him, causing Knox to turn around in surprise.

Marley LaRue leaned against the doorway, her eyes twinkling with mischief as she took in the scene before her. She sauntered over to Knox, the hem of her floral dress swaying with each graceful step.

"Thought I'd come and see what all the fuss was about," she said, her Southern accent wrapping around each word like honey.

"Marley," Knox replied, his voice betraying a hint of amusement. "I didn't expect to see you here."

"Can't let you have all the fun now, can I?" Marley teased, her playful smile tugging at Knox's heartstrings. As they worked together, the chemistry between them

187

was unmistakable, their connection growing stronger with each shared glance and soft laugh.

"Try this," Knox offered, pouring a small sample of his experimental blend for Marley to taste. She took the glass delicately, savoring the aroma before taking a sip.

"Knox, this is...incredible," Marley breathed, her eyes wide with awe. "How did you–"

"Shh," Knox whispered, his finger brushing gently against her lips. He could feel the heat of her breath on his skin, igniting a fire deep within him. "It's our little secret."

As they stood in the dim light of the distillery, surrounded by the scent of the creations, the barriers between them began to crumble. Knox found himself drawn to Marley's warmth and vulnerability, touched by her unwavering loyalty to those she loved.

"Knox," Marley whispered, her voice low and sweet as she reached up to brush a stray strand of hair from his face. Their eyes locked, and for a moment, time seemed to stand still.

Then, as if pulled together by an invisible force, their lips met in a fiery kiss. The taste of bourbon lingered on their tongues, mingling with the passion that ignited between them. It was a connection neither of them had anticipated, yet it felt like heaven.

As Knox pulled Marley closer, their bodies pressed together in an intimate dance of desire, he couldn't help but think that perhaps fate had brought them together for a reason. Love had eluded him for a century, but now, standing in the shadows of the distillery with Marley's warm embrace wrapped around him, he dared to believe that maybe, just maybe, he'd find it after all.

And as the moonlight continued to bathe them in its silvery glow, Knox and Marley surrendered themselves to the passion and mystery that bound their hearts together, forging a bond that would weather even the darkest of storms.

****

Later that night, with the moon high in the sky, casting a haunting glow over the Beaumont estate. A heavy silence hung in the air, thick with anticipation, as Knox and Grayson stood on the veranda, their eyes locked in a serious, silent exchange.

"Have you heard the rumors?" Grayson asked in a hushed tone, his gaze flickering to the shadows that danced beneath the ancient oak trees.

Knox's brow furrowed as he leaned against the railing, recalling the whispers that had circulated through their world about a powerful artifact capable of controlling immortals. "I have, but I'm not sure what to make of it," he admitted, feeling a chill run down his spine at the thought of such a weapon falling into the wrong hands.

Grayson clenched his jaw, the weight of responsibility heavy on his shoulders. "We need to stay vigilant, Knox. If this artifact is real, we can't let it get out and it would cause a war with our kind."

Knox nodded in agreement, his thoughts turning to Marley and the undeniable connection they shared. He couldn't bear the thought of something coming between them, especially after decades of loneliness. "We'll deal with it if and when it becomes a real threat," he said quietly, echoing his brother's determination.

"Right now," Grayson added, his voice filled with conviction, "we focus on the present. We've worked too hard to let anything stand in our way."

With that, the brothers exchanged a nod before making their way back inside the house. They were going to join their friends and loved ones for a night of celebration at the local bar.

The atmosphere in The Greyhound was electric, a mix of laughter, lively conversation, and the clinking of glasses filled with their finest bourbon. Each sip was a testament to their hard work and dedication, the rich flavors dancing on their tongues like liquid gold. It was a moment of triumph, a culmination of passion and perseverance.

Every chance he got, Knox couldn't help but steal glances at Marley, her radiant smile lighting up the room. The sight of her filled him with a warmth that reached down to the very depths of his immortal soul, and he knew he would do whatever it took to keep her safe.

"Come on, Knox," Grayson called out, raising his glass in a toast. "Let's celebrate our success and the bright future ahead before we head out!"

With a grin, Knox raised his own glass, his eyes meeting Marley's as they shared a knowing smile. As they drank to their accomplishments, the thought of the mysterious artifact lingered in the back of Knox's mind, a reminder of the shadows that threatened to encroach upon their hard-earned happiness.

But for now, amidst the laughter and joy of their celebration, Knox allowed himself to be swept away by the magic of the moment, vowing to face whatever challenges lay ahead with the same determination and passion that had brought them this far. Tonight, they would celebrate, tomorrow they could worry about the next problem.

The sultry notes of a jazz melody curled through the air as the group moved around the bar, weaving between the low murmur of conversation and the clinking of glasses. The lively atmosphere was infectious, laughter bubbling up like champagne as friends and strangers alike reveled in their shared passion for fine bourbon. In the midst of it all, Grayson couldn't help but be drawn to the magnetic presence of Raven.

Across the room, Madison leaned against the bar, her light blue eyes sparkling with mischief as she engaged Kenton Wolfe, The Greyhound's bartender in playful banter. "So," she teased, flicking a stray lock of sun-kissed blonde hair behind her ear, "do you always let your bourbon do the talking, or is that just your secret weapon?"

Kenton grinned, running a hand through his own tousled hair. "Well, I find that it helps to break the ice, especially with beautiful women who might otherwise be out of my league."

"Is that so?" Madison's eyes danced with amusement, her lips curling into a coy smile. "I suppose you're lucky that I happen to appreciate a man with good taste in bourbon."

"Nice." Kenton leaned closer, his voice lowering to an intimate whisper as he offered her a glass. "Then allow me to introduce you to something truly exceptional." The subtle brush of his fingers against hers sent a shiver down Madison's spine, igniting a flame of desire she hadn't anticipated.

Meanwhile, Grayson seized the opportunity to pull Raven aside, his intense eyes locking onto hers with a yearning that took her breath away. "Raven," he said, his voice heavy with emotion, "I need you to know how much you mean to me. This life we've embarked on together…I can't imagine facing it without you by my side."

"Grayson," she whispered, her emerald eyes shimmering with unshed tears, "I never thought I'd find someone who could truly see me for who I am, and yet here you are, loving me despite all my imperfections and secrets."

Grayson pulled her close, their lips colliding in a searing kiss, igniting a fierce blaze of desire.

As they broke apart, breathless and flushed, Grayson pressed his forehead against Raven's, his eyes searching hers for reassurance. "I love you, Raven Ballard," he whispered, his voice raw with emotion. "And nothing—not the witches' council or the looming threat of any other thing will ever change that."

"Grayson Beaumont," Raven murmured, her voice thick with emotion, "I love you too. More than you will ever know, my darling."

****

The evening sun dipped below the horizon, casting a warm glow across the crowd gathered at the bourbon review event held on the grounds of the historic Kentucky Grand Distillery. The air was thick with anticipation and excitement as attendees milled around, sampling the various bourbon offerings from both established and up-and-coming distillers. The Beaumont brothers' meticulously crafted bourbon stood proudly alongside Raven's magical Witch's Brew, their unique blends a testament to hard work, dedication, and love.

"Knox," Grayson called out as he approached his brother, who stood pensively near their display, scanning the crowd for familiar faces and potential threats. "You've outdone yourself this time."

"Thank you, Gray," Knox replied, his deep brown eyes flicking to Grayson for a moment before returning to their vigilance. A subtle smile tugged at the corners of his lips, hinting at the pride and satisfaction that lay beneath his stoic exterior.

"Your blend is incredible, Knox!" exclaimed a woman in a striking red dress as she sipped her sample glass. Her eyes widened in appreciation, and she leaned in closer to ask, "What's your secret?"

"Ah, if I told you, it wouldn't be much of a secret now, would it?" Knox responded smoothly, his voice carrying an old-world charm that beguiled those within earshot. He watched as she sauntered away, her laughter echoing through the crowd.

As more attendees sampled Knox's signature blend, their expressions mirrored the woman's delight, and murmurs of praise rippled through the gathering. Each compliment swelled Knox's chest with pride, and he couldn't help but feel a sense of accomplishment wash over him. His tireless pursuit of perfecting the family's craft had finally borne fruit, grounding him amidst the chaos of immortality.

"Knox Beaumont, you have truly outshone yourself," Marley said, her voice soft and filled with admiration as she approached him. Her presence brought a gentle warmth to his thoughts, the unexpected connection between them a balm to his guarded heart.

"Thank you, Marley," Knox replied, his eyes meeting hers with an intensity that spoke of vulnerability and the deepening bond they shared. "Without your support and encouragement, I don't think it would have been possible."

"Let's not forget Raven's Witch's Brew," Grayson chimed in playfully, his eyes sparkling with mischief. "It seems our little witch has a few tricks up her sleeve when it comes to bourbon-making."

"Indeed, she does," Knox agreed, allowing himself a small smile as he watched Raven expertly engage with the attendees, her deep emerald eyes alight with passion and pride for her creation.

As the evening wore on, the energy in the air was pure excitement, igniting the senses and stoking the flames of social acceptance into a very exclusive club. The scent of aging bourbon mingled with the aroma of freshly grilled steaks being prepared for the attendees while sultry jazz tunes played in the background, created a seductive atmosphere that was impossible to resist.

In the midst of the revelry, Knox found himself drawn to Marley, their bodies brushing against one another as they navigated the crowd. The electricity between them crackled with each touch, leaving them both breathless and aching for more. And as the shadows lengthened, the pull of their newfound connection threatened to consume them both, even as they knew the danger it posed to the fragile balance between their worlds, and the friendship they had made.

Raven's fingers traced the rim of her glass, her emerald eyes holding a mischievous glint as she watched the attendees savoring her Witch's Brew. The whispers grew louder, and the crowd around their table swelled. She couldn't help but smile, feeling the pride swell within her as her creation garnered attention and praise.

"Raven, this is absolutely divine," gushed an elegantly dressed woman, taking another sip from her glass. "The blend of flavors is unlike anything I've ever tasted."

"Thank you," Raven responded with a genuine smile, her hair adorned with tiny charms and herbs that shimmered in the dim light. "I wanted to create something unique that honors the magic of our craft."

A sudden hush fell over the room, and Raven's gaze followed the direction of the whispers. A tall man with slicked-back hair and piercing green eyes entered, flanked by two burly bodyguards. Damien Ward, a notorious rival bourbon maker known for his ruthless tactics, had arrived.

"Ah, the famous Witch's Brew," Damien drawled as he sauntered over to their table. "Let's see if it lives up to the hype." He snatched a glass from the table, swirling the liquid before bringing it to his lips. Raven held her breath, her pulse quickening as she watched him closely.

"Interesting," Damien remarked after a moment, smirking at her. "But I'm afraid it's no match for Ward Reserve."

"Your opinion is noted," Grayson interjected, his tone icy and protective, stepping closer to Raven. "But it seems the rest of the guests beg to differ."

"Grayson, let's not cause a scene," Raven whispered, sensing the tension escalating between them. She reached out to touch his arm.

"Of course, my dear," Damien sneered, his eyes roaming over Raven's body with a predatory gaze. "We wouldn't want any…accidents to happen." He raised an eyebrow and turned on his heel, disappearing into the crowd.

Anger simmered beneath Grayson's calm facade, but he forced himself to focus on Raven and her success. "You've done exceptionally well." He brushed a strand of hair behind her ear as his eyes locked onto hers.

"Thank you," she breathed, leaning into his touch.

As the evening wore on, Grayson couldn't help but feel uneasy. Damien's presence had cast a shadow over the review, and he knew all too well that Ward's threats weren't idle. But for now, he would keep his temper at bay and revel in the success of their creations, both Knox's blend and Raven's Witch's Brew. Tonight, they would stand united, letting their passion and determination to carry them through whatever challenges lay ahead.

The warm glow of the chandeliers bathed the opulent ballroom in golden light as murmurs of excitement filled the air. The intoxicating scent of bourbon mingled with the rich aroma of chocolate and spices, creating a sensory symphony that enchanted the senses. Grayson stood at the Beaumont brothers' booth, his piercing eyes scanning the room for any sign of sabotage from Damien Ward and his cronies.

"Grayson," Knox approached, his voice low and steady, "I've been keeping an eye on things. So far, everything seems fine."

"Good," Grayson replied, his gaze never leaving the crowd. "But we can't let our guard down. Not when so much is at stake." His thoughts were consumed by Raven, her emerald eyes and raven-black hair haunting his every waking moment. He couldn't bear the thought of anything happening to her or the success they had all worked so tirelessly for.

As the evening progressed, the atmosphere in the ballroom became charged with anticipation. Attendees eagerly sipped samples of the bourbon offerings, their eyes lighting up with delight as they savored the unique flavors. Among them, Raven's Witch's Brew was garnering its fair share of praise, and Grayson couldn't be prouder of her accomplishment.

"Grayson," Marley whispered, sidling up next to him, "I think I saw one of Damien's men trying to slip something into our batch. We need to do something before anyone else drinks it."

"Damn it," Grayson muttered under his breath. He glanced over at Raven, who was engaged in a lively conversation with Madison and Kenton. She seemed oblivious to the danger lurking nearby. In that moment, Grayson knew what he needed to do.

"Knox, Marley, keep an eye on Raven and the others," he instructed, determination etched across his handsome features. "I'll handle Damien's man."

With swift, silent strides, Grayson crossed the ballroom, his eyes locked on the saboteur. The man had just reached for another vial when Grayson's firm grip closed around his wrist.

"Going somewhere, friend?" Grayson asked icily. Startled, the man tried to break free, but Grayson held him in place with ease.

"Let me go!" the man hissed, fear flashing in his eyes.

"I don't think so." Grayson's grip tightened. In a blur of movement, he yanked the man from the room and into a secluded corridor, shoving him up against the wall.

"Who sent you?" Grayson growled, his voice cold as ice, eyes turning black. The man's gaze darted around nervously, searching for an escape route that didn't exist.

"Damien Ward," he finally admitted under compulsion from Grayson, his voice trembling. "He wanted to ruin her chances at the bourbon review."

"Did you tamper with our bourbon?" Grayson demanded, his anger barely contained, body trembling to release his fangs and end this human.

"No, I swear! I was about to, but you stopped me!" the man cried.

"Good," Grayson said, releasing the man with a shove. "Now get out of here and tell your boss if he ever tries anything like this again, he'll regret it."

As the man scurried away, Grayson returned to the ballroom, calm and collected. He caught Knox's eye and nodded, signaling that the threat had been neutralized. They had overcome this one, ensuring their success remained unmarred by deception.

The tension in the air dissipated, replaced by a sense of camaraderie and unity among their friends. Laughter filled the room as they celebrated their achievements, raising their glasses in a toast to hard work, friendship, and victory.

"Here's to us," Grayson declared, his eyes meeting Raven's as she smiled at him from across the room. "To our success, and to the bright future that awaits us all."

The celebration continued, the room buzzed with laughter and chatter, the air charged with triumph. Grayson's gaze lingered on Raven, watching as she gracefully sipped her drink, her eyes shining with satisfaction. He could feel the heat of desire building within him, a fire stoked by the way her raven-black hair framed her delicate face. And the way that dress hugged her body, he was not sure how much longer he could control his desire for her.

"Hey, Grayson," Knox said, leaning in close to his brother, "I overheard something interesting while I was getting a refill."

"Really?" Grayson raised an eyebrow, his curiosity showing. "What's that?"

Knox glanced around before continuing, his voice hushed. "Someone mentioned that the artifact rumors might be more than just idle gossip. Apparently, there have been a few…incidents lately that suggest someone is trying to find it."

"Interesting," Grayson mused, stroking his chin. Could this new challenge be related to their recent conflict? Were they about to find themselves drawn into a web of intrigue involving the mysterious artifact?

"Let's keep our ears open and stay vigilant," Grayson suggested, his mind racing with possibilities. Knox nodded in agreement, and they clinked their glasses together in a silent pledge.

The moment had arrived for the announcement of the winners. The judges stood, collecting their notes and exchanging hushed words. A ripple of anticipation ran through the crowd, all eyes fixated on the small group preparing to reveal the results of the bourbon review. A silent exchange passed between the two brothers as their eyes met briefly.

The head judge cleared his throat, commanding silence. "Ladies and gentlemen," he began, his deep baritone permeating the grand room, "we have tasted some truly excellent bourbons tonight. The competition was fierce, but two distilleries have emerged as clear winners."

The room seemed to collectively hold its breath as the judge continued, "In second place..." A pause for dramatic effect had several attendees leaning forward in anticipation, "... Witch's Brew Distillery!"

A round of applause echoed through the room as Raven beamed with pride, her emerald eyes sparkling with joy under the twinkling lights. She graciously accepted the accolades, her gaze seeking out Marley and Madison in the crowd. Their shared smiles were radiant, a testament to their tireless efforts and unyielding friendship.

"And in first place," the judge's voice boomed once more through the tense silence that followed, "we have Beaumont Bourbon Distillery!"

For a nanosecond, shock froze Knox and Grayson in place before an elated cheer escaped from them. The room erupted in cheers and congratulations as they stepped forward to accept their victory. It was a triumph not just for them but for their family legacy—an affirmation that they were more than mere immortals; they were guardians of a time-honored tradition and craftsmen of unparalleled skill.

Amidst this jubilation, Marley found Knox's eyes. His joy reflected in her own gaze that twinkled with mischief and warmth. As though magnetized by an unseen force, they gravitated toward each other. The world seemed to fall away, leaving only them in the heart of the celebrating crowd.

"Congratulations," she said, her voice dripping in

southern sweetness through the victorious commotion around them.

"Thank you," Knox replied, his deep brown eyes locking onto hers. "Could not have done it without your support, Marley."

Then, as if time slowed, they leaned into each other. The air between them crackled with electricity as their lips met in a passionate kiss.

As the celebration roared on around them, they savored their shared moment of victory and the sweetness that was all their own. Tonight was a night filled with victories—for their legacy, for their friendships, and for love…A beacon of hope amidst the dark complexities of their supernatural lives. A promise that no matter what challenges lay ahead, together they were invincible.

On the other side of the room, Raven leaned against Grayson as they shared a private moment amidst the buzzing crowd. His arm around her waist felt secure and inviting.

"Raven," Grayson said, his voice low and seductive as he spoke to her, "I can't help but think about how incredible you look tonight. It makes me wonder what it would be like to explore every inch of you."

Raven's cheeks flushed, her breath hitching at his words. Her eyes locked onto his, a mixture of surprise and anticipation swirling within their depths. "Grayson," she whispered, her voice quivering, "we can't…not here. It is forbidden in such a place."

"Ah, but the forbidden has always held such allure for us, hasn't it?" Grayson countered, unable to resist teasing her. He revealed in the way her body responded to his, the undeniable chemistry between them surging like a storm.

"Maybe we should discuss this somewhere more private?" Raven suggested, her voice breathy and laced with desire.

Grayson's heart thundered in his chest as he took her hand, leading her away from the celebration and out the front door.

"Let's go home then." Grayson's eyes smoldering with a hint of desire.

Raven nodded, her heart hammering in her chest as she allowed him to guide her. The night air was cool against their flushed skin as they stepped outside, but the heat between them was burning her alive inside. They slipped into Grayson's sleek black car, the hum of the engine mixing with the throbbing pulse of their own anticipation.

"Are you sure you want to leave the party early?" Grayson asked, his voice gentle yet laced with passion.

"I've never been more certain about anything," Raven responded, her voice resolute.

As they drove down the winding country roads, the Beaumont estate came into view. The light from the house spilled out onto the lush lawn, casting long shadows that danced beneath the ancient oak trees. Grayson pulled up to the front door, his hands steady despite the pounding desire coursing through his veins.

Hand in hand, they entered, and as soon as the door closed behind them, all pretense was forgotten. Grayson swept Raven into his arms, passion igniting like a wildfire between them. Their lips met in a heated exchange, tongues exploring with a hunger only matched by their bodies' desperate clamor for each other.

****

Back at the celebration event, Knox and Marley savored their shared triumph and burgeoning romance. Unbeknownst to them, their passionate encounter had not gone unnoticed. Madison watched from across the room, a knowing smile tugging at her lips as she clutched an untouched glass of bourbon.

Catching sight of Madison's knowing glance, a blush crept onto Marley's cheeks, but she held her ground, her feelings for Knox too strong to ignore. She made her way through the throng of jubilant guests toward Madison, who raised an eyebrow—part amused and part intrigued—at her approaching friend.

"Madison," Marley started hesitantly as Madison interrupted her, holding a hand up and grinning slyly, "don't. I saw the kiss. And it's about damn time."

Marley giggled. Emboldened by her best friend's acceptance, she glanced back at Knox, who was now talking to some of the guests, a faint smile playing on his lips. It was a night of celebration after all—for love, friendship and most importantly, the legacy they were resurrecting. Unseen threats be damned, tonight they basked in joy and triumph.

As the moon hung high over Bourbon County, casting everything in a silver glow, Marley rested her head on Knox's shoulder. They sat in silence under the twinkling lanterns, letting the fading sounds of celebrations lull them into a peaceful reverie. Their new romance had just begun and already they could feel it seeping into their bones like the finest of bourbons—intoxicating and irrevocable.

"Marley," Knox whispered into her hair as he held

her close, "I want to show you something."

Taken by surprise but intrigued, Marley allowed herself to be led away by Knox as the predawn hours broke over Bourbon County, heralding not only a new day but also a promise of many shared dawns to come between them. Little did they know that this night was only the beginning of their fascinating journey together, full of mystery, passion, and the allure of the forbidden.

As they ventured from the party and back to the Beaumont estate, Knox could feel Marley's curiosity peaking. They passed the main house as he led her to the back of the grounds. She looked around in wonderment at the lavish garden and towering trees that encapsulated their silent voyage. Her hand fit perfectly within his—a comforting warmth that had him yearning for more intimate connections.

"Knox," Marley began, her voice barely above a whisper. "Where are we going?"

"We're almost there," he replied cryptically. The anticipation in her eyes was irresistible, making Knox wish he could hold onto this moment forever. "Just a little further."

Finally, they reached their destination—an old wooden cabin nestled deep within the woods. It was a serene sanctuary away from the bustling world, where Knox would often escape to when he needed solitude. Tonight, however, he wished to share this haven with Marley.

"This is your secret hideaway?" she asked in awe as they stepped inside. The space was warm and welcoming, with an undeniable rustic charm. It was intimate and personal—an insight into Knox's world that made Marley's heart flutter with delight.

"Yes," Knox confessed, his eyes never leaving hers. "And I've never shared it with anyone before."

The declaration left Marley speechless. She understood the significance of his words and couldn't help but be touched by his vulnerability. This was not just a physical place; it was a sacred part of him—a piece of his immortality that he had always kept hidden…until now.

They spent the rest of the night wrapped up in each other's arms, talking about dreams and hopes, fears and secrets. As dawn approached, they found themselves lost in a kiss—a soft surrender to an allure they could no longer deny.

Knox's cabin became an altar of adoration for the two of them. They explored one another not just in body but also in spirit - opening doors they never knew existed. Under the soft glow of candles flickering rhythmically to the tune of their whispers, they poured out dreams that had been hibernating in the recesses of their hearts. A connection was forged in silence; a bond sanctified by shared dreams and mutual respect.

****

Back in the main house, Grayson and Raven were lost in their own little world of passion. Their bodies intertwined like vines, seeking warmth and support, their breaths merging in a rhythmic dance. The boundaries between them blurred, and all that existed was the raw, primal connection that tugged at their souls, refusing to be denied.

Every brush of skin, every whispered confession, set their senses alight. Raven traced a path along Grayson's jawline—rugged and firm as the man himself—eliciting a rumbling growl from deep within him. Responding to this tantalizing provocation, he slipped his hand into her raven locks and brought her in for a kiss so passionate it made the world dissolve around them.

****

Back at the party, Madison continued her flirtation with Kenton under twinkling lanterns, their laughter echoing off into the distance. Madison's golden hair reflected the vibrant life she brought to any gathering.

The night drew on, each couple retreating into their worlds of newfound passion and promise. Unknown to them all, it was an evening that was just the beginning—an overture to a grand symphony of love and mystery that Bourbon County had yet to witness.

Underneath the joy, worry remained that their world would be shaken. Their lives would change in ways they could have never foreseen. But for now, though, they basked in their newfound love and shared dreams- a beacon of hope against the darkness that was surely awaiting to descend upon them.

When the morning light filled every corner of Bourbon County, after a night of secrets shared and love declared, six souls intertwined prepared themselves for whatever fate would throw their way. Together they stood stronger; together they would face the unknown. And though uncertainty hung heavy in the air, so did a promise of love stronger than time itself.

Chapter 11

The warm, golden sunlight bathed the grand Beaumont estate, highlighting the vibrant gardens where lively conversation and laughter floated on the breeze. The group had gathered for an outdoor lunch. It was an intoxicating ambiance that seemed to create a lively energy among the gathered companions.

Glasses clinked together and the aroma of rich Kentucky bourbon perfectly complemented the tantalizing scent of the dishes being served. The laughter and chatter from the guests painted a picturesque scene of tranquility, calmness blanketing their lives for now.

The magic-infused land around them seemed to hold its breath, as if understanding the gravity of these moments and the implications it held not just for Raven and Grayson, but also for everyone who had become entwined in their story. Their lives would never be simple—together they would build something extraordinary.

Grayson leaned against one of the wrought-iron tables on the patio, his piercing eyes scanning the scene as he took in the joy radiating from every corner. His hair fell in effortless waves, framing a face that was equal parts mischief and allure. He couldn't help but feel a sense of contentment as he watched everyone enjoy each other's company, their bonds deepening with each shared moment.

"Grayson, you've truly outdone yourself, my friend," Marley drawled, her Southern accent thick with approval as she approached him. Her striking auburn hair framed her expressive eyes, which seemed to sparkle with warmth and amusement.

"Thank you, darlin'," Grayson replied, his voice dripping with charm. "Nothing but the best for my favorite people."

As the group continued to chat and laugh, Grayson's gaze lingered on two new couples who had recently found happiness within their circle. The first pair consisted of Marley and his amazing younger brother, Knox, whom he was so happy for. Their affection for one another was evident in their every interaction—the way they exchanged sly glances when they thought no one was looking, or how their fingers brushed against each other's as they reached for their drinks.

The second couple was Madison and her newfound love, Kenton. Their connection was like a wildfire, passionate and all-consuming. The blonde-haired Madison often leaned in close to Kenton, her eyes dancing with curiosity as they engaged in animated conversations. Their laughter rang throughout the garden, infectious and full of life.

"Seems like we've got quite the lovebirds among us, huh?" Grayson mused aloud, his gaze flitting between the two couples.

"Love is in the air," Marley agreed with a playful wink. "And speaking of lovebirds, where's our dear Raven?"

"Right here," Raven replied as she gracefully

joined them at the table, her hair cascading down her back like a dark waterfall. Her deep hypnotic eyes met Grayson's gaze, and he could see the depth of emotion that lay just beneath the surface.

"Raven," Grayson murmured, his voice low and intimate as he reached out to brush a strand of hair from her face. Their fingers lingered, a silent spark igniting between them, a moment that seemed to stretch into an eternity, shared with a look that spoke volumes of unspoken longing.

A playful nudge from Marley broke the spell, and both Grayson and Raven laughed as they returned to the easy banter and conversation that filled the sun-drenched afternoon. But as the laughter continued, Grayson couldn't help but steal glances at Raven, his thoughts consumed by the powerful emotions that coursed through him whenever she was near.

The sunlight dappled through the trees, casting a warm glow on the table laden with an abundance of delicacies, from succulent roast meats to vibrant, fresh salads. The fragrances of rosemary and thyme mingled with the rich aroma of bourbon, setting the scene for a perfect afternoon feast. Grayson watched Raven as she laughed at one of Knox's jokes, her emerald eyes sparkling like precious gems. His heart swelled with a mix of anticipation and nervousness as he thought about the surprise he had planned for her.

"Hey, Gray," Marley leaned in and whispered, breaking him from his reverie, "you look like you're a million miles away. Nervous about something?"

"Maybe just a little," Grayson admitted, taking a sip of his bourbon to steady his nerves. "I've got something special planned for Raven, and I want it to be perfect."

"Knowing you, I'm sure it will be," Marley reassured him with a smile.

Grayson had spent countless hours preparing for this moment, studying ancient texts to find the perfect spell that would create an enchanting evening for them both. He had even ventured deep into the woods to collect rare herbs and flowers, whose petals shimmered with iridescent colors that seemed to dance in the moonlight. As the sun began to dip lower in the sky, he knew that the time was drawing near.

"Raven?" Grayson said, his voice betraying a hint of vulnerability. "Could I speak with you alone for a moment?"

"Of course." She followed him toward a secluded spot beneath a grand old oak tree.

Once they were alone, Grayson took a deep breath and began to recite the incantation he had painstakingly memorized. As the words flowed from his lips, the air around them seemed to hum with energy, the very atmosphere crackling with anticipation.

"Grayson, what are you—" Raven began, but her words were cut off as a sudden gust of wind swirled around them, lifting the petals he had collected into a dazzling whirlwind of color. The world seemed to blur and fade away, leaving only Grayson, Raven, and the mesmerizing display of shimmering petals that danced like fireflies in the twilight.

"Raven," Grayson said, his voice barely clear above the rustle of leaves and the whispers of the spell. "I wanted to create something magical for us, a moment where we could be together without any distractions or fears."

Raven stared at him, her eyes wide with wonder and disbelief as the last of the petals settled around them like a soft, fragrant blanket. "This is incredible, Grayson," she breathed, reaching out to touch one of the still-glowing petals. "How did you—"

"Magic, your dad taught me," Grayson replied with a grin, pulling her close and capturing her lips in a searing kiss that sent shivers down her spine.

As their bodies pressed against each other, the electric charge between them grew stronger, their hearts beating in perfect synchrony. Time seemed to slow down as they lost themselves in the intensity of their connection, every caress and gasp heightening the passion they shared.

"Raven," Grayson whispered into her ear, his breath hot against her skin. "My love for you knows no bounds, and I would do anything to make you happy."

"Grayson," she murmured, closing her eyes as she leaned into his embrace, letting the magic of the evening enfold them both in its warm, inviting glow.

As the last remnants of their passionate kiss lingered on Raven's lips, Grayson pulled back slightly, his eyes filled with a tender vulnerability that contrasted with his usual confident demeanor. The glowing petals surrounding them seemed to mirror the intensity of his emotions, casting an ethereal light on their entwined forms.

"Raven," he began, his voice low and hesitant, as if searching for the right words. "I know we come from different worlds, and our future together may be uncertain, but I am certain of one thing: I want you by my side for as long as time allows."

His penetrating blue eyes locked onto hers, a storm

of emotions swirling within their depths like ocean waves. "Would you…would you consider becoming my wife one day?" Grayson asked, his voice barely above a whisper.

The question hung in the air between them like a fragile thread, threatening to shatter the delicate balance they had built. Raven's heart raced in her chest, a mixture of joy and nerviness coursing through her veins as she grappled with the enormity of his proposal.

"Grayson…" She breathed, her eyes widening with surprise and delight. And yet, her mind was already racing, considering the implications of such a commitment. Their love was forbidden by nature as it was, their lifespans so vastly different. Could they truly build a life together under such circumstances? Their worlds so different, their paths destined to diverge eventually, but in the moment, they were intertwined in destiny's dance. As she looked into his hopeful eyes, her fear still hung on. What if he changed his mind one day? Then she would die alone and heartbroken, for her marriage was a onetime deal.

"Are you sure about this?" she asked, her voice trembling ever so slightly. "You're immortal, and I'm not. There will come a time when I'll grow old, and you'll remain unchanged. How can we possibly face that?"

Grayson's gaze never wavered, his eyes filled with determination and devotion. "I know the challenges we face are unlike any other," he replied, his voice steady and strong. "But I believe that our love is powerful enough to conquer these obstacles. We may not have an eternity together, but let's make the most of the time we do have."

"Grayson," she whispered, tears glistening in her eyes, "I love you more than anything in this world, and if you're willing to face those challenges together, then yes…I will consider becoming your wife."

A radiant smile spread across Grayson's face as he pulled her tightly against him, sealing their promise with a searing kiss that spoke of their unbreakable bond. As they stood there, surrounded by the magical glow of the enchanted petals, Grayson slipped a black diamond ring on her finger.

Grayson and Raven returned to the group, their faces beaming, sharing their news as cheers filled the air and tears of joy overcame everyone. Jubilant laughter and warm congratulations filled the air. Marley, her eyes shining with happiness and unshed tears, enveloped both Raven and Grayson in a bone-crushing group hug, her petite frame surprisingly strong.

"Y'all did it!" she exclaimed, pulling back to gaze at them with elated awe. "I haven't seen two people more suited for each other in all my life!"

"Yay!" Madison chimed in, a huge smile plastered over her beautiful face.

Raven chuckled at her friends' enthusiasm, running a finger over the black diamond now adorning her finger. The gem glittered under the sun, a tangible testament to their shared promise.

Grayson, meanwhile, watched them with a smile that reached his eyes, his hand absent-mindedly tracing soothing circles over Raven's back.

As the night wore on and the jovial spirit of their celebration deepened, a familiar sense of calm washed over them. Their lives would never be exactly normal—

after all, they were intricately intertwined in an otherworldly realm replete with magic and immortality—but they had found solace in their shared destiny.

Even as whispers of a powerful artifact continued to circulate and the delicate balance between their supernatural world and the human one threatened to unravel, they knew they could face it. For they were stronger together than they could ever be alone, their bond forged in the flames of love and sealed with an unbreakable vow.

****

There was a hum in the air with an undercurrent of tension as the group gathered around the long oak table. Their laughter and chatter masked an undercurrent of worry that clung to them like morning fog.

"Has anyone heard anything else about this artifact?" asked Marley, her voice steady, but eyes filled with concern.

Grayson glanced at Raven, his fingers brushing hers beneath the table, before breaking his silence. "I've been doing some research, and it seems that every time this artifact has surfaced throughout history, chaos has followed."

"Chaos?" Morgan raised an eyebrow, his deep eyes searching Grayson's face for answers. "What kind of chaos?"

"Rumors say it can grant its possessor immense power," Grayson explained, his voice tinged with apprehension. "But no one knows for sure what it does or how it works. All we know is that those who seek it tend to leave destruction in their wake."

Raven squeezed Grayson's hand, her thoughts

shifting to their recent commitment and the uncertainty it brought. She struggled to ignore the nagging fear that the artifact could pose an unforeseen threat to their future together.

"Whatever this artifact is, we need to make sure it doesn't fall into the wrong hands," she said. "If it truly is as powerful as they say, then we must protect our family, our legacy, and our town."

"Agreed," chimed in Knox, his gaze flitting between Grayson and Raven. "We can't let anything come between us, especially not something as unpredictable as this artifact."

"Then we will deal with it head-on," declared Grayson, his voice unwavering. "Together, as a family, we will ensure the safety of those we love and the world we've built."

Their makeshift family nodded in unison, a sense of camaraderie bolstering their resolve. Despite the complexities of their relationships and the looming threat of the artifact, they knew they could rely on each other to face this.

"Let's make a pact," proposed Marley, her voice resolute. "No matter what happens, we stand by one another, facing every challenge and danger as one."

"Agreed," murmured Madison, her hand gripping Grayson's in solidarity.

"Agreed," echoed Knox, his gaze lingering on Marley for a moment longer than necessary.

"Agreed," whispered Raven, her voice sweet but her heart swelling with courage and determination.

"Agreed," affirmed Grayson, his eyes locked on Raven's.

As the group raised their glasses in a solemn toast,

their commitment to one another and any battle that awaited them solidified, forging an unbreakable bond between them all.

****

The sun was setting over the lush Kentucky landscape. It was in this tender twilight hour that the group found themselves gathered on the veranda of the Beaumont estate, sharing stories and laughter as they reveled in the beauty of their surroundings. The air was thick with the scent of honeysuckle and freshly cut grass, mingling with the subtle undertones of aging bourbon from the nearby distillery.

"Remember when we first met?" Marley mused, her eyes dancing with mischief as she glanced around the circle of friends that had become her family. "Who would have thought we'd end up like this?"

"Bound together by love, magic, and a good measure of bourbon," Madison replied with a wry smile, raising her glass in a toast to their enduring bond. A chorus of agreement accompanied the clinking of glasses, punctuated by Knox's deep chuckle.

"Love is a powerful force," he murmured, his gaze flitting briefly to Marley before returning to his drink. "It can break through even the strongest barriers."

Grayson watched the exchange from the corner of his eye, feeling a mixture of gratitude and protectiveness toward those who had grown so dear to him. They had been through so much together, in such a short time—passion, heartbreak, and now the looming threat of the artifact—yet they remained steadfast in their commitment to one another.

"Here's to us," Grayson declared, lifting his own glass in salute. "To the love that binds us, and the friendships we have by our side."

"Cheers!" echoed the others, their voices filled with warmth and sincerity as they drank to their shared journey.

As the conversation continued, Raven's hand slipped into Grayson's, their fingers intertwining with a natural ease that still sent shivers down his spine. He turned to her, drinking in the sight of her flushed cheeks and the way her emerald eyes sparkled in the fading light.

"May I steal you away for a moment?" he asked, his voice barely above a whisper.

"Of course," Raven replied, her smile soft and inviting as she allowed him to guide her away from the others.

They found solace beneath a canopy of ancient oak trees, their gnarled branches casting dappled shadows on the ground below. Grayson drew Raven close, pressing a tender kiss to her forehead as they swayed gently in each other's embrace.

"Sometimes, I can't believe how far we've come," he murmured, his breath warm against her skin. "From that first meeting at the estate, to now...I never imagined I could find such happiness."

"Neither did I," Raven admitted, resting her head against his chest. "Our love has given me strength I never knew I possessed, and a family I didn't think I'd ever have."

Grayson tightened his grip on her, his heart swelling with pride and affection for this extraordinary woman who had captured his soul. As they returned to their friends and family, hand in hand, both bearing radiant smiles, it was clear they were prepared for their next chapter. The tale of Grayson and Raven was far from over, but they would face the future as one.

"Here's to a new beginning," Marley toasted, raising her glass with a warm smile. Everyone followed suit, their glasses clinking together in a symphony of hope and love.

Yet in the midst of this joyous occasion, the truth remained: an ancient artifact was still at large, looming like a dark cloud threatening to disrupt their newfound peace. The future was uncertain, fraught with mystery and danger. But with the power of their love and the strength of their bond, they were ready to meet whatever challenges lay ahead.

****

The following weeks settled into a comfortable rhythm, with Grayson and Raven learning to navigate their new reality. The smile that graced Grayson's face each time he looked at her only intensified, and the black diamond ring on her hand gleamed unnervingly in the light.

Marley threw herself into the role of wedding planner with fervor, bringing a touch of much-needed levity to the proceedings. Her infectious enthusiasm lifted their spirits and filled their days with laughter and countless discussions about flower arrangements, cake designs, and everything else down to the minutest detail.

The group fell into a soothing routine, each enjoying what life had brought them. New friendships, success, joy and love. They kept moving forward, just like life in central Kentucky rolled on like the timeless hills surrounding them.

And so ended one enchanting chapter in their

lives—a story of passionate love intertwined with an ageless mystery within the bluegrass. Yea, their lives would not abide by normalcy's rhythm, carrying the centuries-old intrigue of immortality, a blend of bourbon legacy and supernatural secrecy. And…despite the current calm, an undercurrent of unease lingered in the air, whispering of the tempestuous storms yet to come.

A word about the author...

AD Curtis, a devoted mom from Kentucky, lives with her two amazing sons and her beloved fur baby. Her passion for reading ignited a desire to write from a young age. After years of nurturing this dream, she is now turning it into reality with her debut book, blending imagination and heart into every page.

Thank you for purchasing
this publication of The Wild Rose Press, Inc.

For questions or more information
contact us at
info@thewildrosepress.com.

The Wild Rose Press, Inc.
www.thewildrosepress.com